THE MURDER AT SISSINGHAM HALL

An Angela Marchmont Mystery Book 1

CLARA BENSON

MOUNT
STREET
PRESS

MOUNT
STREET
PRESS

ClaraBenson.com

Cover concept by Yang Liu
WaterPaperInk.com

Cover typography and interior book design by Colleen Sheehan
WDRBookDesign.com

Print spine and back cover design by Shayne Rutherford
DarkMoonGraphics.com

Chapter One

I T IS ALWAYS a very odd feeling, returning to one's home country after a long period abroad. The countryside, the towns, the cities, people going about their daily business, even the weather, look familiar and yet at the same time strange. It reminds me of the feeling I once experienced on accidentally observing myself in a looking-glass which had been placed at right-angles to another—it was quite a shock to see a reflection of my reflection and suddenly realize that my true face was all lop-sided. When I got my first glimpse of the quayside from the deck of the *Ruthin Castle*, a welcome sight after the long voyage, a jolt of joy went through me, yet at the same time I felt oddly shy, like a small boy made to stand up in the drawing-room and recite poetry before a gathering of stern aunts.

'No-one will be here to welcome me,' I thought to myself, as the vessel drew ponderously into Southampton dock. 'I am like a stranger in my own country. Shall I be able to settle down, I wonder?'

The gang-plank went down and I disembarked with the rest of the passengers, alone in the midst of a teeming mass of humanity. For a moment I stood on the quayside, my feet on English soil for the first time in eight years, discomposed by the bustling crowd of passengers, sailors and porters and momentarily uncertain as to which way to go. But just as I was heartily beginning to wish that I had remained in South Africa, I heard a piercing whistle through the din and, turning my head, saw two figures weaving with difficulty towards me. My heart leapt. I was not a stranger after all.

'Bobs!' I cried. It was indeed my oldest friend, 'Bobs' Buckley, accompanied by a rather good-looking girl I didn't recognize. I had written to Bobs, informing him of my impending return but I had been far from expecting him to come and meet me. I started forward.

'Bobs! How marvellous to see you,' I said, beaming, as I wrung his hand. 'I had no idea you intended to come and meet me. I thought I should have to slink up to town all alone like a disgraced relative.'

'Think nothing of it, old chap,' said Bobs, with a grin. 'Couldn't let an old friend down. Thought we'd give you a surprise. As a matter of fact, your return has come at just the right time. I've been wanting to try out the Lagonda on a straight run, just to see what she can do. My word, you should have seen her fly!'

'Oh! I know I shall never recover from the fright. I'm certain my hair has turned completely white,' cried the girl. 'Bobs, I'm sure you ran over that cat in Winchester.'

'A mere bump in the road, I assure you,' said Bobs airily. 'In any case, it would serve it right if I had run over it. A cat has no business getting in my way when I am in a hurry.'

'Silly!' said the girl, exasperatedly. 'How was your trip, Charles? Was it too terribly ghastly? Where are your things? Bring the bags along please,' (to the porter). 'By the way, you are coming back to Bucklands with us, aren't you? I mean, I suppose you don't have any immediate business in town? Mother and Father are very much looking forward to seeing you.'

'I—I—' I said, confused by this torrent of speech and puzzled as to which question to answer first. Before I could answer any of them, it dawned upon me suddenly who she was and I started in surprise.

'Sylvia!' I exclaimed. 'I hardly recognized you. Good heavens! I had no idea you had grown up. Have I really been away that long?'

When I had last seen Bobs's sister, she had been an ungainly schoolgirl with a grubby face and a reckless disregard for the state of her clothes; quite different from the smart, fashionable young woman standing in front of me now. I could not help staring at her, astonished at how much she had changed. She flushed slightly and pulled a face, which immediately brought to memory the tom-boy she had once been and I laughed.

We all stood there for a few moments, grinning foolishly at each other as the crowd flowed around us, then Bobs said:

'Better get going then, if we're going to make it back to Bucklands at any time today.'

'Oh, yes,' sighed Sylvia. 'I suppose I shall have to risk life and limb once again. I simply *insist* that you come back with us,' she said, linking her arm through mine and turning towards a monstrous, dark-green contraption that could only be Bobs's latest motor-car, 'Otherwise I shall have to listen to Bobs's piffle all the way back to Bucklands.'

'Rot. You know perfectly well that I speak only words of the utmost wisdom. I say, isn't she a beauty, Charles?' said Bobs, eagerly. 'I've never had a car like her. On a clear stretch of road she can easily do eighty miles per hour.'

Having duly expressed my admiration, I was permitted to climb in. Once the baggage was safely installed and the porter suitably remunerated, we set off at breakneck speed, narrowly missing an elderly gentleman and a nurse pushing a pram. It was clear that Sylvia had not been exaggerating when she had spoken of Bobs's driving skills.

'I see that you are still seeking out danger wheresoever it may lurk, Bobs,' I remarked, as we reached the London road and the powerful motor-car began to eat up the miles. Bobs shrugged.

'You know how it is. I never could seem to settle back into things after the War. I should have liked to join the Air Force but Father wouldn't hear of it. Not after Ralph died, you know.' Ralph was Bobs's elder brother, who had been killed at Arras. 'So I confine myself to more sedate activities.' He looked as though he were about to say something more but then thought better of it.

I made some reply and tactfully changed the subject.

Sylvia had, understandably, preferred to sit in the back seat. I turned round and complimented her on her new-found elegance.

'It seems only yesterday that you were putting frog-spawn in my pockets,' I said. 'But how you've changed! You are quite the *chic* lady. I hardly know what to say.'

Sylvia accepted my compliments with great composure.

'Oh, Sylvia still puts frog-spawn in people's pockets,' Bobs assured me. 'Only last week there was very nearly an embarrassing incident with the American Ambassador during cocktails. Luckily, Rankin came to the rescue just in time. I really don't know what we'd do without Rankin. In fact, I shouldn't be at all surprised if Father disinherits me and adopts Rankin as his heir. There's no doubt he deserves it more than I.'

'Well, I'm sure he doesn't go around running over people's cats,' said Sylvia.

'Of course not! He's far too solemn and lugubrious for that. I say, isn't "lugubrious" a marvellous word? And it fits Rankin to a nicety. No, I can't see him running over cats but I can imagine him wringing their necks as a hobby,' he continued darkly. 'Perhaps if we went into his room we should see them hanging around the walls like bunting.'

'How absurd you are, Bobs! As you can see, Charles, he hasn't changed a bit. Neither have I, really. I'm just a little more polished these days, now that Rosamund has taken me in hand.'

Too late, Bobs shot her a warning look, as a thrill ran through me.

'Rosamund?' I inquired. 'Rosamund Hamilton?'

'Rosamund Strickland now,' corrected Sylvia.

'Yes, of course, I forgot. Has she been giving you lessons in dress and deportment? Picking up handkerchiefs and all that, what?'

'Not exactly. A couple of years ago when she was down at Bucklands, I happened to admire her clothes and she insisted on introducing me to her dressmaker. You know Mother —she is rather vague and much happier grubbing about in the garden in tweeds, so it was quite a relief to find someone who really takes an interest. One receives so many invitations these days and I was quite floundering, as it was no use begging Mother to take me up to town. Luckily, Rosamund came to the rescue. She knows all the best places to go and Mother was quite happy to relinquish the responsibility. Look out!' she said, suddenly, as Bobs swerved to avoid a pheasant.

As she and Bobs argued, I was silent, deep in thought. It had come as a shock to hear Rosamund's name mentioned so soon after arriving back in England and now I examined my feelings closely, not wholly able to make them out. Certainly, I admitted to myself, I should not have been surprised to hear about her—she had always been part of our 'set' in the old days and there was no reason why she should not have remained so, especially since I had left England shortly after our engagement came to an end. It was hardly reasonable to expect her to stop seeing my friends once I was out of the picture; in fact it sounded pretty much as though she and Sylvia had become bosom pals in the meantime. Rosamund was not the reason for my leaving the country—so I had always told myself, but was that true? At any rate, there was no use in regretting how things had turned out, as she had married at almost the same time as I left and I—well, I had found myself with other things to worry about in that harsh, unforgiving heat.

So I reflected, then smiled to myself as I decided that the romantic feelings I had once had for Rosamund had long since disappeared. In fact, it would be rather nice to see her again. After all, she had always been a most charming woman, with the ability to make a chap feel like the wittiest and most attractive man in the room. Tired and jaded though I was, I was looking forward to getting back into things and showing the world that while experience might have battered me a little, it had certainly not beaten me and that I was ever the man I had been.

The rest of the journey was uneventful and as we turned in at the lodge gates of Bucklands, Bobs threw me a sideways glance.

'All right, old man?' he asked. I knew what he meant.

'All right,' I replied, smiling.

'Here we are. It's not much but it's home,' he said, as we drew up in front of the stately pile that had been the seat of the Buckleys since the Restoration or thereabouts, so it was claimed. The Buckleys were an old, old family that throughout the ages had survived and prospered by shrewdly backing the right side during times of strife, marrying into the right families and sending its sons into Parliament to pursue long, worthy careers. The present generation was no exception.

I received a quiet yet sincere welcome from Lord and Lady Haverford, whom I had always considered as a second family, my own having been so unhappy in so many ways. I was shown to a warm, comfortable room and urged in the friendliest manner to remain at Bucklands for as long as I liked.

We were a gay party that evening, talking nineteen to the dozen, recalling old times. My sun-tan was remarked upon and I was begged most flatteringly to recount some of my adventures abroad which, I must admit, were not as thrilling as I should have liked. Not for me the daring, dangerous life of a true pioneer or a big game hunter. I had left England to take up a respectable post running a farm; subsequently, finding farming a disappointment, I had tried mining and as luck would have it, had struck gold—literally—almost immediately. Much of my time abroad had therefore been taken up with the day-to-day running of my business. Fortunately, my adventures were enough to entertain my audience and Lord Haverford in particular intimated that he would like to pursue talks further at a later date, on a more business-like footing.

Despite my tiredness after the long journey, we talked late into the night, until, one by one, the various members of the family were overcome by sleep and went up to bed. At last, only Bobs and I remained, sitting in companionable silence in two easy-chairs set one each side of the fire. I watched Bobs as he stared at the flames. He had not changed a bit: still the same knowing smile and easy laugh, always with a ready joke to enliven and lift the spirits of any party. In his earlier youth, he had ever been a source of worry to his family, given his unfortunate liking for tearing about town with a succession of unsuitable young women. I wondered if he had mellowed at all.

Bobs looked up and caught me smiling.

'I was just thinking of the old days and wondering whether you are still causing your parents' hair to turn grey,' I explained.

He laughed.

'Yes, I was rather a rapscallion, wasn't I? Mother lived in constant terror that I would run away to Paris and marry an opera singer. Mind, it was a close thing sometimes. Do you remember Lili Le Sueur?'

I remembered her only too well. Bobs had met her when she was dancing in the chorus of one of the lesser productions. For professional purposes she claimed to be French, although in reality she was an American with laughing eyes and an enormous sense of fun.

'I should say so. But I seem to recall that it was all over between you by the time I left England. Didn't she return to America?'

'Yes. She wanted to star in pictures, she said, but I heard that she married a dentist back home in Wisconsin. I suppose she has got fat and lost her looks by now,' said Bobs regretfully. 'That's the worst of these married women. They settle down and get caught up in domestic cares and then they are not worth looking at any more.'

I found myself wondering whether Rosamund had lost her looks and was vexed with myself. Why should it matter? I must be tired after the journey, I thought, or I would not be giving in to such weakness. Rosamund was part of my past and I was keen to embrace the future.

'So have you given up consorting with unsuitable young ladies?' I asked, half-jokingly.

Bobs did not answer immediately. He seemed absorbed by the fire, or possibly by thoughts of the enchanting Miss Le Sueur. I repeated my question and he started.

'Eh—what's that? Oh, yes, I have done with all that kind of thing. I am older now and get into a different kind of scrape.'

There was a strange look in his eye. I glanced questioningly at him but he did not elaborate. Instead, he continued to stare wistfully into the glow.

Nothing remained of the fire but smouldering embers and I was starting to feel the chill of an English October after my years in the sun.

'I think I had better go to bed,' I said, standing up and stretching. 'It is simply splendid to see you again, Bobs. I can't tell you how grateful I am that you came to meet me at Southampton. I was looking forward to a night in a dreary hotel in London but how much pleasanter it is to spend my first evening among friends!'

Bobs waved my thanks away airily.

'Go and get a good night's sleep, old chap, and dream of the veld.'

I bade him goodnight and climbed wearily up the stairs to my room, where I found my things neatly unpacked and laid out for me. Undressing quickly, I fell into bed and soon drifted off into a deep sleep untroubled by any dreams at all.

CHAPTER TWO

I SPENT SEVERAL days with the Buckleys, joining them in the usual country pursuits and round of social events that are generally attached to a great house such as Bucklands. After such a long time away, I was surprised to find how easily I fell back into the old way of things. The heat and dust, the sounds and the smells of Africa began to seem like part of a previous life and after only a few days, I ceased to feel like a foreigner in my own land. Bobs and I spent several enjoyable days fishing in the stream that ran through Bucklands Park. In the evenings there were cocktails and parties, while on the rare occasions on which there were no visitors, we all talked and laughed together late into the night.

During that week, I also spent some time getting re-acquainted with Sylvia—or rather, getting acquainted with the lively young woman she now was, instead of the mischievous child she had once been. We passed endless hours walking around the grounds; she asking me intelligent questions about the life of a gold-miner and making me laugh with amusing tales of her friends in London, who seemed rather a wild crowd. I found her very good company and I sensed that she liked me too. My mind wandered into idle speculations of a most pleasant nature. I supposed I ought to be thinking of settling down before I became too set in my ways and Sylvia was the sort of girl I had always been attracted to: pretty, clever and sympathetic. Furthermore, I was sure that I would encounter no opposition from Lord and Lady Haverford. Despite misfortune, my family background was considered almost impeccable and now that I had become a successful man in my own right, their minds would certainly be relieved of any lingering doubts. I drew back from making any firm commitment, however, reflecting that I had only just returned to England and that I had no wish to act precipitately or take an irrevocable step that I might regret.

'You seem rather preoccupied, Charles. What are you thinking about?' asked Sylvia, looking sideways at me as we strolled around the rose garden, taking advantage of a short spell of autumn sunshine after several days of drizzle. I roused myself from my musings.

'How rude of me. I'm afraid I let my mind stray to business matters,' I replied. 'It seems I have not yet shaken off the cares of the world, which can be my only excuse for letting my attention wander.'

'Oh dear! Well, we simply must try and bring you out of yourself. You were rather stern and reserved when you first arrived but a few days have already done wonders for you. But we can still do better. Bobs and I are going down to Sissingham Hall to visit the Stricklands in a couple of weeks. You must come with us. I shall get Rosamund to invite you.'

I must have hesitated, because Sylvia immediately blushed, put her hand to her mouth and cried:

'How simply dreadful of me, I completely forgot! Of course, you can't have seen Rosamund since—'

Feeling, for my own sake as well as hers, that I must reassure her quickly, I laughed as naturally as I could and told her not to be an idiot.

'Rosamund and I are old friends, nothing more,' I said easily. 'Our engagement was a mistake and both of us quickly realized it. We parted on the best of terms and I should be very happy to see her again after all these years.'

Sylvia had been watching me intently as I made this not-entirely-truthful speech and seemed relieved.

'I'm glad of it,' she said. 'I was afraid I had said the wrong thing. I'm always doing that. Mother says I shall never make a diplomat's wife.'

Again I told her not to be silly and instructed her in no uncertain terms that she was by no means to avoid Rosamund's name; that I was looking forward to seeing Rosamund again; and, moreover, that I also relished the prospect of renewing my acquaintance with her husband, Sir Neville Strickland. I further intimated that there were other women—a woman even—whom I found more attractive these days. Sylvia quite rightly snorted at this thunderingly clumsy attempt at gallantry but seemed satisfied with my assertions.

'Anyway,' she said, reverting to the topic of my self-improvement, 'I hope you are planning to stay with us for a good while yet. I—we are very much enjoying having you here. And besides,' she continued in a practical tone that was more like herself, 'You won all my money last night and I want to win it back.'

I laughed and we argued the point all the way back to the house.

'What were you two talking about so cosily in the rose garden?' Bobs murmured to me with eyebrows raised, as we came in to tea.

'Haven't you anything better to do than to watch people strolling in the rose garden?' I replied blandly. Bobs's eyebrows rose further but he did not press the point.

'Charles, dear boy,' boomed Lord Haverford as he entered the room. 'We must have that chat about the prospecting rights. I have the maps all prepared.'

'I'm ready now, sir, if you like.'

'Then let's go to my study, where we won't be disturbed. As for bringing someone else into the business, I know the very man. Have you met Sir Neville Strickland? He already has interests in Africa and knows the work.'

Sylvia looked up warily and I couldn't help but catch her eye as I was conducted out of the room. I smiled brightly and she gave me a wink, much to Bobs's evident entertainment. I felt a little guilty for leaving her to withstand Bobs's merciless teasing alone but Lord Haverford was not to be refused. And anyway, I reflected, she must surely be used to it by now.

After a week or so of more or less idle enjoyment, I reluctantly felt I must go up to London. I had business awaiting me there and, more pressingly, I was finding that my light clothes were wholly inadequate to ward off the chills of a dank October. So, dressed in a warm suit lent to me by Bobs, I arrived at Waterloo station for my first encounter with the fogs of London in more than eight years. After the ruin and subsequent death of my father, I had left town almost a pauper, owning little more than the clothes I stood up in; now, as I hailed a taxi and pronounced the words: 'The Ritz', in emphatic tones, I experienced a certain feeling of jubilation, for which I think I can hardly be blamed.

Once I had firmly installed myself and my belongings in that luxurious establishment, the next few days were spent in conducting essential business. I very soon possessed myself of a suitable wardrobe and as I surveyed myself in the long glass, I noted with satisfaction that, apart from the sun-tan, no longer could I be immediately set down as a Colonial. The next step was to set inquiries afoot for a discreet valet: I had lived in the rough for long enough and now I was determined to avail myself of all the comfort and convenience that London life affords. Of course, I would also have to find somewhere to live but that was not yet an immediate concern.

Town was rather quiet at that time of year but I managed to look up a few old school-mates, who were very glad to see me, or gave every appearance of it, and saved me from the unspeakable dullness of spending each evening alone. I dined out, disported myself rather disgracefully at the newest and most fashionable jazz night-clubs, danced with a string of pretty women and generally shook the dust of South Africa from my feet altogether.

Shortly after my arrival in London, I received a letter from Sir Neville Strickland, inviting me to lunch at his club with a view to discussing the prospecting rights. He rose and shook my hand warmly as I was ushered in to the grand, wood-panelled room in which so many vital affairs of state had been discussed over the years—and so many questionable deals done.

'Delightful to see you again, my boy,' he said. 'It must be five years since you left, what?'

'Eight, sir,' I replied.

'Indeed? So long? My, how time flies! Well, well, let us sit down. What will you have? The fish here is very good.'

Sir Neville was a florid man of around fifty, who was much more at home in the country than in town. He made cursory inquiries about my recent return to England, then plunged straight into the business at hand. This lasted us all the way through to coffee, when he suddenly changed the subject and invited me down to Sissingham Hall.

'We should be very happy to see you,' he said. 'I know that Rosamund particularly wishes you to come, since you are such old friends. Young Buckley and his sister will be there and one or two other people. I expect it will be quite a jolly party. What do you say, hm?'

I accepted his invitation with thanks and promised I would play my part in making it a lively weekend. I had no idea when I said it that this would turn out to be truer than I had supposed.

'How is Rosamund?' I inquired.

'Oh, she's splendid, splendid. Of course, she finds it terribly dull in the country, so she's very keen on these house parties. Naturally, I leave it to her to do all the organizing. Women are much better at that sort of thing, don't you know. We men do well to stay out of it!' He gave a short bark of laughter.

I well remembered how Rosamund used to bask in the gay brilliance and glitter of a large party, with herself as the queen of the evening. She had an almost child-like delight in being the centre of attention and would repay the devotion she received by graciously bestowing notice on her worshippers, rewarding them with dazzling smiles and a few moments in the bright circle of her radiance. I had been one such acolyte myself for a short while but this time I would resist.

The conversation touched on sport and fishing and then turned to politics and public affairs. Sir Neville bemoaned the rising costs of running his estate and became quite heated on the subject of tax. I nodded and made sympathetic replies whenever called upon to do so, although in truth, I was not really listening. I was instead reflecting on the strange forces that bring people together. Sir Neville and his wife were two very different people, with apparently very little in common: he was a staid, middle-aged man, strongly attached to the countryside and much preferring a tranquil life and family surroundings, while she was a lively, beautiful young woman with a wide circle of friends and a taste for excitement—and yet by all accounts, they were a devoted couple whose mutual attachment nobody doubted. But perhaps Rosamund had altered in the eight years since I had last seen her. Time wreaks many changes, as I knew only too well.

Sir Neville and I parted with cheery salutations on both sides; he to return to his Norfolk estate and I to my suite at the Ritz, where I had some letters to write. On my return, I found a telegram waiting for me. It read:

Hope Neville remembered to invite you Sissingham. Do come. Will not be the same without you. Strong silent Colonial simply essential to complete party.

I could not help but smile. However else she might have changed, it appeared that Rosamund was still as impulsive as ever.

Two days later, I happened to wander into a restaurant which was well-known among certain circles for its discretion and caught sight of Bobs dining with a rather striking-looking woman. They seemed to be having a private conference and I was just about to ask tactfully to be seated well away from them, in order to avoid causing embarrassment to all concerned, when Bobs caught my eye and beckoned me over.

'Hallo, old chap,' he said. 'Come and join us. We were just talking about Sissingham. Have you met Mrs. Marchmont? Angela, this is my great friend Charles Knox. Angela is Rosamund's cousin. She's been living in America but now she has returned to England and is coming to Sissingham next weekend. Try not to let the fact that she dines with disreputable types such as I put you off, by the way. She is a woman of impeccable reputation and delightful company to boot.'

Mrs. Marchmont took this pleasantry with good humour.

'How do you do, Mr. Knox,' she said. 'As Bobs says, I'm afraid you catch me at a disadvantage. Still, I suppose that is the way society is going these days and you know in the States we take these things much less seriously, which must be my excuse!'

She gave a wide smile and shook my hand as she spoke. I must say I rather took to her immediately. Tall, dark-haired and dressed elegantly but not ostentatiously in shimmering blues and greens, she appeared no more than thirty at first glance but a closer look revealed one or two lines about the eyes and the mouth that told a different tale. She was not precisely beautiful but there was a certain look in her eye that attracted and yet challenged. I had heard about Rosamund's American cousin of course, and remembered vaguely that they had been close as children but had not seen each other since Mrs. Marchmont left England. The waiter drew up a chair for me and I sat down.

'How long were you in America?' I asked politely.

'Oh, longer than I care to remember! Why, it must be fifteen years, now I think about it,' she replied. 'I went out there a year or two before the War. And yet, now I have returned, it seems only yesterday that I left.'

She told me about her delight in meeting Rosamund again, after so many years apart. As children they had been almost like sisters but circumstances had separated them and she was looking forward to getting reacquainted with her cousin, of whom she spoke with great fondness.

Mrs. Marchmont seemed to be on the most friendly terms with Bobs, which did not surprise me, as Bobs knew everyone.

She had had many interesting experiences in America and made some intelligent observations about how things had changed in England since she left. In this respect, we had much in common, both of us having spent time away from our native land and seeing it for the first time in many years from the perspective of outsiders.

Mrs. Marchmont did not remain with us for long, as she had an engagement elsewhere. I escorted her to her car.

'It has been very nice to meet you,' she said, as the car drew up. 'I look forward to continuing our conversation at Sissingham.'

I assured her that the feeling was mutual and watched for a moment as the motor pulled away. It struck me that Mrs. Marchmont was very different from her cousin. Then I returned to our table, where Bobs was just lighting up a cigar.

'A fine woman, that,' he remarked. I could not help but agree with him.

'Rather inscrutable, too, perhaps,' I said. 'She appeared to me to be quite unlike the average woman who has an interest only in jewellery and fine dresses. You may think it odd but while we were talking, I had the strangest feeling that she held many secrets and could reveal a great many interesting things if she chose.'

'Yes, she does strike one that way, doesn't she?'

'Is there a Mr. Marchmont? She didn't mention him at all.'

'Why, I couldn't say. I believe there is, or was. A financier, or a captain of industry, or something like that, back in America.'

'From what she said, it sounded as though she and Rosamund were as thick as thieves, once.'

'Yes, that's true—despite the age difference,' Bobs said. 'Angela is rather older than Rosamund, you know. I believe she has always been fiercely protective of Rosamund—especially after the trouble happened with old Hamilton. But Angela's family weren't exactly well-to-do either and she had to make her own way in the world, so they parted. She was a secretary to some Duke or other and then took a post with Bernstein, the financier. That's how she ended up in America. Rosamund was still a child at that time and she stayed in England with her mother and grew up with very little money—but of course you know about all that.'

I did indeed. When my own father had been ruined, throughout all the misery and difficulties that ensued I had at least felt, for a short time, that Rosamund and I had something in common. But it soon became clear to me that I could not expect her to live in poverty with me. Despite her penniless childhood, Rosamund was not a person whom one associated with saving and scrimping. One could not imagine her cheerfully ordering the cheapest cuts from the butcher, or darning socks, or washing the plates on the maid's day off. When one pictured Rosamund, it was in a grand, elegant, warm setting, surrounded by brightly burning lights and dressed in glittering array. No, the rough-and-ready life of South Africa, the struggle for existence, the uncertainty of the future—they were not for her.

'Tell me about Sissingham,' I said. Bobs waved his cigar vaguely.

'Oh, it's comfortable enough, I suppose. A bit on the small side but it has some jolly good shooting. Miles from anywhere, of course.'

I took the comment about the house's size with a grain of salt, knowing well that Bobs judged all buildings against the standards of Bucklands.

'Sylvia spends quite a bit of time there, doesn't she?' I asked.

'Yes, she and Rosamund are great pals these days. In fact, we both go to Sissingham quite often. The Stricklands are fond of entertaining—at least, Rosamund is. Neville less so.'

'What do you mean, less so?'

Bobs grinned.

'Oh, he'd much prefer to sit by his fireside or work alone in his study every evening. He puts a brave face on it but Rosamund has the upper hand of him there. I mean, dash it, you can't marry a good-looking woman like that and keep her all to yourself, can you?'

'Do they spend a lot of time in town?'

'Not as much as Rosamund would like. That's why they have so many house parties, to keep her from getting bored.'

'Do you know who is coming next weekend?'

'I believe it is to be a smallish party. Apart from us and Angela, the only other guests will be the MacMurrays. I don't think you know them. Hugh MacMurray is a cousin of Sir Neville.'

'MacMurray—MacMurray. I don't recall the name.' I frowned, trying to remember.

'No? Well, you'll meet them soon. He's a nice enough chap but I wouldn't trust him with anything important. His wife is a rather interesting woman.'

'In what way?'

Bobs smirked knowingly and lowered his voice to a confidential whisper.

'She has come up in the world these days but I knew her slightly when I was going around with Lili. Just be sure not to believe anything she tells you about herself. I shan't say any more.' He gave an exaggerated wink.

I sat back in my seat.

'Bobs, you really are the most frightful old gossip!' I chided. 'You are quite an old woman. I'm half-ashamed of myself for listening to such rot!'

Bobs disclaimed my epithet with a grin.

'No harm in a little idle chatter. I'm sure you will find her a fascinating woman. She has a certain charm about her, in her own way. In fact, what with the MacMurrays and your seeing Rosamund for the first time since you left England, it promises to be a most interesting weekend.'

I thought this a rather malicious attitude and told him so with dignity. Deep down, however, I felt that he could be right.

CHAPTER THREE

I T WAS A chill, crisp autumn afternoon when I stepped down from the slow train at the tiny station of Tivenham St. Mary and squinted into the fast-sinking sun. Sir Neville had said that somebody would be there to meet me but the place seemed deserted. I picked up my bags, waving away the porter, and came out of the station. Nobody was about but as I drank in the clear evening air after the choking fumes of London, I heard an engine in the distance and, turning, saw a motor-car approaching down the road. It pulled up alongside me and an inquiring face in horn-rimmed spectacles peered out.

'Hallo. You must be Mr. Knox,' it said.

I assented. The inquiring face alighted from the car. It was attached to a slightly-built young man with a self-effacing manner.

'I am Simon Gale, Sir Neville's secretary. He has sent me to collect you. I do hope you haven't been waiting long, only I was running a little late, I'm afraid.'

'Not at all. The train arrived only a few minutes ago,' I said. 'I have been enjoying the fresh air.'

'Oh good,' he said, relieved. 'Are those your bags? Here, let me take them for you.'

He stowed them safely.

'Hop in. It's not too far, although it's quicker if you walk over the fields,' he said and moved off with a crashing of gears. 'Have you been to Sissingham before?'

'No, never,' I replied. 'But I understand it is a beautiful place.'

'Yes, it is—a delightful old house. It is surrounded by very fine countryside, too.'

'Have you been there long?'

'About a year and a half. I count myself very fortunate to have found this post. Sir Neville has been very kind to me. Of course, he has his humours, like anyone but—' he stopped abruptly and reddened, perhaps fearing that he had said too much, 'but I have never been happier than since I took up this post at Sissingham.'

'A glowing testimony indeed!' I said, wondering what he meant by 'humours'.

We trundled along the country road, with Gale pointing out noteworthy landmarks here and there. It certainly seemed a remote enough district: there was hardly a building to be seen for miles around. If one wanted to cut oneself off thoroughly from the rest of the world, then this was surely the place to do it.

As I sat there, half in a day-dream, I was jolted awake by the sudden roar of an engine. I looked round and saw a familiar, dark-green motor-car looming up behind. Although the road was too narrow by far, it moved out to pass us.

'Good God! What's that?' cried Gale, as he swerved violently to the left to avoid a nasty scrape. As luck would have it, the road widened slightly at that point and we narrowly avoided ending up in the ditch. The green Lagonda shot off into the distance with a roar.

'If I am not mistaken, *that* is Mr. Buckley and his sister,' I said breathlessly, resolving to give Bobs a piece of my mind later.

'Oh, dear me! Oh, dear me!' said Gale. He was slumped over the wheel and looked quite white and shaken.

'Come now, man, it's only Bobs,' I said, in an attempt to cheer him up. 'You ought to count yourself lucky that you are in this car, not that one. If you were in Bobs's car, you would really have reason to worry. He is a menace to the countryside.' I meant it jokingly but Gale was shaking his head, trembling.

'I'm sorry, Mr. Knox but I have not been well, not been well at all,' he repeated wanly. 'My nerves, you know. I'm afraid sudden loud noises quite startle me.'

This seemed to me something of an understatement but I could understand now why a post in such a quiet, faraway spot should have appealed to him.

'Well, they've passed now,' I said. 'Let's get on. Are you all right?'

'Yes, yes thank you. I feel much better now,' he replied and indeed the colour was slowly starting to return to his cheeks.

'I'm sorry I reacted so badly but I'm afraid that since my illness I am quite unable to stand any degree of noise and much prefer peace and quiet.'

'Oh quite, quite,' I said breezily, in an attempt to gloss over the uncomfortable moment. 'And you have picked a perfect spot for it.'

We set off again and reached the gates of the park without further mishap. Sissingham Hall was set in the very centre of the park, with views in all directions. The building itself was a mish-mash of styles. The original building dated back to Elizabethan times, Gale told me, but very little of it was left, as successive owners had knocked down some parts and added others. Overall, the result was not unpleasing and the house seemed to blend in harmoniously with the landscape.

We drew sedately up to the front entrance and got out. My heart was beginning to beat in my mouth and I steeled myself against the imminent first encounter with Rosamund. Instead, however, we were greeted at the door by a lumpish, sulky-looking girl I didn't recognize, who was attempting to keep two skittish terriers under control.

'You must be Mr. Knox,' she said abruptly, holding out her hand. 'Rosamund is resting in her room, but Bobs and Sylvia are in the drawing-room. I don't know where Neville is—he was in a foul mood earlier. I'm Joan Havelock, by the way. Mind the dogs, or they'll trip you up.'

Startled at this blunt greeting, I followed her into the grand entrance hall, managing with difficulty to avoid the terriers, who were barking delightedly and indeed seemed to want nothing more in life than to send me flying headlong. Joan

Havelock led me to a large, well-appointed drawing-room, where a few people were already gathered. Bobs was standing in the window, talking to a woman I didn't know. He turned and greeted me with a sheepish grin.

'It's no use you shouting at me, Charles,' he said, before I could speak. 'I've already been firmly taken to task by Sylvia.'

I tried to assume a disapproving demeanour but as ever, it was impossible to remain cross with Bobs, so I gave it up as a bad job.

'No lasting harm done. We were just a little shaken up,' I replied. 'Only to be expected when one careers into a ditch.' I decided to remain quiet about Simon Gale's attack of nerves, as I had no wish to embarrass him further.

'Well, a cocktail will soon put you right,' said Bobs, as a tray approached, laden with drinks. He turned to the woman. 'Gwen, I don't believe you've met Charles Knox. Charles, this is Gwendolen MacMurray.'

'Delighted to meet you,' said Mrs. MacMurray. She drained her glass, took another cocktail, held out her hand to me and gave me an appraising look from head to foot, all in one fluid movement. 'I understand you're a gold-miner, Mr. Knox. Tell me, what was Africa really like? Is it really as dangerous as they say? My husband wanted to go into mining some time ago but one hears such stories about the heat and the animals and the natives, that really I couldn't bear to think about it! I simply couldn't have put up with it and of course Hugh wouldn't hear of going without me, so in the end it came to nothing. But sometimes I wonder whether it mightn't have been better if we had gone. One hears of simply enormous fortunes being made out there in the gold fields.' She sighed. 'Why does making money have to be such hard work? It seems terribly unfair to me.'

Bobs gave a shout of laughter.

'Isn't she precious, Charles? Gwen would like to spend her days surrounded by rich furs and jewels and be waited on hand and foot by a phalanx of devoted admirers. She makes no secret of the fact.'

Mrs. MacMurray pouted a little.

'I don't see any harm in wanting nice things. Lots of people have nice things and I want to be one of those people, that's all. I should hate to have to live in a small house, with nothing to eat and no servants.'

As I looked at her, it struck me that there was little likelihood of that. Gwendolen MacMurray was plainly a woman who knew what she wanted. She was exquisitely turned out in what, even to my untrained eye, was undoubtedly the height of expensive Parisian fashion and was almost festooned with strings of jewels. Her face held a sort of doll-like beauty and I suspected that both it and her immaculate blonde hair owed not a little to the art of the salon. She was leaning towards me confidentially and swaying slightly and it was quite evident that she had already had several cocktails. Bobs, meanwhile, had wandered off to talk to Miss Havelock.

'Is this your first visit to Sissingham?' she asked. 'Hugh and I come several times a year. Hugh's mother was Sir Neville's cousin, you know and Hugh is his closest living relative. In fact,' she continued, lowering her voice, 'Sissingham Hall will pass to Hugh if the Stricklands have no children.' She paused and gazed glassily over my shoulder for a moment. 'Of course, Sissingham is a beautiful old place but I don't think I should like to live here all the time, so far from London. Perhaps we could sell it. Then we could have a house in London and spend the rest of the year in Monte Carlo, or perhaps Juan les Pins—no, I think Monte would be nicer. One sees more interesting people there.'

I was conscious of a faint feeling of distaste. I wanted to extricate myself from the conversation but I was pinned into the corner next to the window. Worse was yet to come, as a new idea dawned, tearing Mrs. MacMurray away from her visions of future riches.

'Of course! I remember your name now!' she exclaimed loudly. 'Weren't you engaged to Rosamund at one time? Somebody—who was it now?—told me that it all ended between you and you went off to Africa with a broken heart. You poor dear boy! You know, I think that's simply too romantic. It's very brave of you to return here, isn't it? I should love to have two strong men fighting over me. In fact,' she continued confidentially, in a lower tone, 'there was a time when I could have had my choice of men to marry, but then I met Hugh and that was that.'

She clasped her hand to her bosom and tottered slightly. I cast my eyes wildly around the room, hoping for a means of escape and saw Bobs standing very near, smirking. He was clearly enjoying my discomfiture enormously and made no attempt to rescue me. My salvation came at last with the entrance of Sir Neville and a man I took to be Mrs. MacMurray's husband, Hugh. If Sir Neville had indeed been in a foul mood, as Miss Havelock had said, he seemed to have got over it, as he was smiling broadly.

'I'm so glad you could come,' he said as he joined us. 'I'm sorry I wasn't here to greet you but some urgent business cropped up—you better than anyone know how these things happen. But I see Gwen has been entertaining you. Gwen, my dear, are you feeling quite well? You look a little peaky.'

Gwen made a visible effort to pull herself together.

'Thank you, Neville, I'm quite well apart from a slight headache. I think it must have been the long journey. I'll lie down for a little when we go to dress but I'm sure I'll be quite all right.'

Given her interest in Sissingham, Gwen MacMurray obviously had no wish to disgrace herself in front of Sir Neville and the change in her manner was striking. After our conversation only a few minutes before, I was astounded to see her cast down her eyes so modestly and reply to our host in such a graceful fashion. She seemed almost a different person. My mind went back to Bobs's hints about her past and it occurred to me that perhaps she had once been on the stage. She was certainly an impressive actress.

I took advantage of Sir Neville's arrival to edge away from Gwen and found myself being introduced to Hugh MacMurray, her husband. I supposed that women would consider him a good-looking man, although there seemed to me a touch of weakness about his mouth, which his moustache could not quite hide. He asked the usual questions about Africa and about how I was settling into life back in England.

'Must be quite a change, what? Shooting pheasant in the rain instead of lions on the plain.' He roared at his own wit. 'As a matter of fact, we nearly went out to Africa ourselves a couple of years ago but Gwen funked it at the last minute. Didn't want to move so far away from her friends. Or from the Paris fashion-houses.' He roared again. 'When I meet fellows like you, who have made their fortunes out there, I sometimes wonder if I oughtn't to have insisted. Still, can't complain. It's a good life, all in all and I wouldn't swap Gwen for all the gold in the world.'

I noticed that he looked continually towards his wife as he spoke and wondered if he could possibly mean what he said. Gwen caught his eye and moved across to join us.

'Now, Boopsie,' she said. 'I hope you have been playing nicely with Mr. Knox and haven't been boring him too much. He is *such* a naughty boy, you know,' she said, turning to me. 'Sometimes he is really quite impossible, aren't you my sweet?' She reached up and tweaked his moustache.

MacMurray's countenance had assumed the aspect of a hypnotized sheep.

'Just as you say, dear,' he said, gazing fondly upon his prize.

Mercifully, Gwen was just then claimed by Sylvia and Joan, who wanted to talk about frocks or some such nonsense and she moved away. To my great relief, MacMurray's expression returned to normal and he resumed the conversation as though nothing had happened.

'Your wife seems a very—remarkable woman,' I said, for want of a better adjective.

'Oh she is, she is,' he replied. 'I don't mind admitting that I was a bit of an old rogue before I met her but I am quite the reformed character now. In fact, there's no greater champion of the married state than I. Gwen is quite wonderful. You have seen for yourself how charming she is. She is one of those rare women who is a great favourite with the men without attracting the jealousy of other women. I probably shouldn't say this,' he continued confidentially, 'but I get rather a kick out of seeing her flirt with other men and be admired by them. Some chaps wouldn't allow that kind of thing but I'm not the jealous type myself.'

I was quite at a loss as how to reply to this but just then we were joined by Sylvia, so I was spared the necessity. She dispatched MacMurray to fetch her a cocktail.

'Thank goodness it's you!' I exclaimed in a low voice. 'I was beginning to feel as though I were caught up in a scene from *Alice in Wonderland*, or something of the sort.'

Sylvia smiled.

'Are the MacMurrays too much for you?' she said. 'I'll admit that they are an acquired taste.'

'That is certainly one way of looking at it,' I replied. 'But how exactly does one acquire the taste without getting sick? I have only just arrived and yet I already feel as though I have had a surfeit!'

She laughed and I noticed how her eyes gleamed in the dimming light.

'Come now, you're just tired and grumpy after the long journey. You are showing all the signs of a man who wants his dinner—I know them well. You will feel much better after you've eaten, you'll see!'

'Perhaps,' I conceded. 'Tell me, who is the Havelock girl?'

'Oh, didn't she introduce herself? She is Neville's ward.'

'She didn't seem very friendly.'

'Yes, she can be rather shy and awkward in company but she is very nice when you get to know her. I think she feels a little overshadowed by Rosamund, to tell the truth. She is quite witty though and much cleverer than I am.'

'Impossible!' I returned, mockingly and she threw me a reproving look.

Simon Gale silently entered the room and drifted over to where Sir Neville was standing with Joan. Mrs. MacMurray was exerting her considerable charm on Bobs by the French windows.

Hugh MacMurray returned with Sylvia's drink and began talking of the latest theatre productions. I left them to it and moved over to the group in the corner. I felt I ought to pay my duty to my host.

'Look, here's Mr. Knox, come to entertain us,' said Joan. In Sir Neville's presence, she seemed to be making more of an effort to be polite to the guests.

'I don't know about that,' I said, in mock alarm. 'In fact, I was feeling frightfully dull myself and was rather hoping that you would entertain me.'

She laughed and her face was transformed.

'Actually, we were talking about the weather! This is what happens when one sees the same people every day, you know. One has to resort to chewing over the same old subjects.'

'But, my dear, since we have guests here and may wish to take them around the grounds tomorrow, the weather is of the first importance,' said Sir Neville, not unreasonably.

'I suppose so, although you know that you would happily go tramping about the countryside every day, come rain, shine, hail or snow, especially if there was any shooting to be had.'

'I might, certainly but I can hardly insist my guests do the same.'

'Do you shoot?' I asked Simon Gale and was not surprised when he shook his head in reply.

'It is not a sport that appeals to me,' he said. 'I am not very dexterous with a gun.'

'I wish you would take a day off once in a while and come shooting,' said Sir Neville. 'I never knew such a fellow for working day after day at all hours.'

'I enjoy my work,' replied Gale mildly.

'Neville can't understand why anybody wouldn't want to go out shooting every day,' said Joan. 'He's a positive fiend with a shotgun.'

'You exaggerate, my dear but I confess that I like to get out as much as possible. There is something about being out in the fresh air that causes one to forget one's troubles, if only for a short while.'

Joan snorted.

'Troubles, indeed! Really, Neville, what troubles can you possibly have?'

'There speaks the voice of youth and irresponsibility,' I interjected lightly, as I saw that Sir Neville's face had darkened. Joan ploughed on, laughing.

'Why, nobody has less right to claim a troubled life than Neville! He's rich, with a lovely house and a beautiful wife. He can do whatever he wants.'

'I only wish that were so, my dear,' said Sir Neville, recovering himself. 'But when you are a little older you will come to realize that even the most fortunate of us can have our problems.'

Whether because of the tone of his voice, or for some other reason, Joan made no reply and a short, uncomfortable silence descended. It was broken by Sylvia, from the other side of the room.

'Whatever can have happened to Rosamund?' she exclaimed. 'She only went to speak to the cook about dinner but she's been simply *ages*.'

For a short while, in the flurry of new acquaintances, I had completely forgotten about Rosamund but now my heart began to thump again—mostly at the thought of the whole party's being witness to our first meeting in eight years.

'I'll go and see where she's got to, shall I?' Joan said and moved towards the door. Just as she did so, however, it was flung open and two people came in. I recognized one of them as Angela Marchmont. The other was Rosamund.

Chapter Four

THE ROOM FELL silent and everyone turned to watch as Rosamund paused in the doorway and scanned the assembled company, as though seeking someone. Then she caught sight of me and let out a little scream.

'Charles, darling!' she cried, heading straight towards me and clasping both my hands in hers. 'How simply divine to see you again! My, how well you look! Sylvia, you sly thing, you never told me how delightfully handsome he was looking!'

'I can't say I'd noticed,' replied Sylvia carelessly.

'Nor had I,' I admitted. Everybody laughed and the moment of tension was broken. The buzz of conversation resumed.

'Come and sit by me here and we shall have a nice cosy chat before dinner,' said Rosamund, pulling me over to a Chesterfield at the far end of the room. 'I won't share you with anybody else. Rogers, bring me a drink. Now, Charles, you simply must tell me all about your adventures since I last saw you. Is it true that miners pay for everything in gold nuggets out there? And how many leopards have you shot? It must have been simply thrilling!'

Although I had answered the same questions time after time in the course of the preceding weeks—and had become pretty tired of hearing them, to tell the truth—Rosamund had a way of saying the same old things that somehow made them sound witty and fresh and, more importantly, made one feel rather pleased with the cleverness of one's own replies. I found myself telling her all about my early struggles on the farm, how I had gradually realized that farming was not for me and how, just as I had almost determined to chuck it all in dejectedly and return to England with my tail between my legs and no hope of enrichment, I had fallen in with an old-timer at the Colonial Hotel, leathery of face and rheumy of eye, who had taken a fancy to me, induced me to buy him a whisky and whispered in my ear that he knew where gold was to be had and was looking for someone young and strong to help him claim it. The old fellow died just as we had begun to attain success, which I was heartily sorry for, for he had been good to me, but I buckled down and determined that his faith in me should not prove to have been misplaced. Several years later, I surveyed my achievements with satisfaction and decided that it was time to withdraw from the day-to-day running of the business and return to England to enjoy the fruits of my labours.

To me the whole episode seemed rather dull and prosaic, a history of eight years' unremitting hard work, but Rosamund seemed to find it fascinating and listened to my tale wide-eyed, with occasional gasps of astonishment. I began to feel that perhaps my story was not so dreary after all and felt myself puffing up rather. That was always the thing about Rosamund, though: something in her manner always made one feel rather complacent about oneself.

'But I am afraid I have been boring you,' I said. 'I've done nothing but talk about myself. Now you must tell me what you have been doing.'

'Of course you haven't bored me!' exclaimed Rosamund. 'Why, I can't remember ever being so enthralled by someone's life story. No-one around here has such marvellous tales to tell. Certainly not me, in any case. No, Charles, I'm afraid you only have to look at me to see what I have been doing these past eight years—I have become a respectable married woman and grown fat and middle-aged. I seem to find another grey hair every day!' She laughed and complacently tossed the offending mass of shining red-gold, which gave the lie to her assertion.

I knew Rosamund of old and knew she was perfectly aware that she had not grown in the slightest bit fat and at twenty -eight could hardly be described as middle-aged. One thing Rosamund had always been certain of was her power to captivate and the mirror would surely have told her that she was looking as lovely as ever. She looked like nothing so much as the cat that had got the cream. I said as much and she shrieked with laughter.

'Oh, you can't think how I've missed you, Charles!' she said, clasping my hand. 'You always did know how to put me in my place. Whenever I was feeling terribly dignified and full of myself you would look at me in that sidelong way of yours and say something devastating and yet screamingly funny, so I would simply collapse in a heap of laughter. You never took me at all seriously, now admit it!'

'I never take anything seriously,' I said, feeling rather rakish.

'Well you must have taken your business seriously, or you couldn't have done so well as you have. Tell me, are you *terribly* rich?'

'Oh, terribly. In fact, I have so much money I shall never be able to spend it all. What would you recommend I do with it?'

'I can think of lots of things. I never have enough money myself—if I did I should give you plenty of examples of how to spend it!'

'Not have enough money! Of course you are joking.'

'Joking! Perhaps I am a little. I suppose one ought to be thankful for what one has but really, it is so easy to run through it that sometimes I am almost afraid to show Neville my cheque-book at the end of the month. I confess that I am a little extravagant at times.' She admitted this so ruefully and yet so charmingly, that I felt that Sir Neville must consider it practically an honour to pay her bills.

'So, then, tell me how you would spend my riches for me,' I said, jestingly.

'Oh! Well, I should have a big house in town, of course, and throw lots of parties. You would be astounded, Charles, at how much it costs to be the toast of the season! One can fritter away simply oodles of cash.'

'Don't you already have a house in town?' I asked, surprised. Rosamund shook her head regretfully.

'We did in the beginning but Neville said it was costing him too much to run and he didn't like it anyway. He's never been fond of living in London you know, so we moved here more or less permanently and I am reduced to being a guest in other people's houses when I want to gallivant.'

'Do you miss it?'

'Sometimes. Mainly in spring. Sissingham is beautiful but it is rather far away from everything. I refuse to let Neville bury himself here in the country all the time, however. We still do Deauville and Cowes and all those places. One can't be a martyr to all things, you know!'

'I should have thought you would hate leaving town. I expected that you would become a grand society hostess and hold glittering balls that would pass into legend.'

She did not reply immediately and when I looked at her I saw she had turned her face away. But when she turned back to me and spoke, her expression and tone were normal.

'So did I! But you know, as we grow older we find that what we actually want is not always the same as what we thought we wanted. Oh dear, I seem to have tied myself up in knots. Did that make sense? Neville and I are very happy and I wouldn't change things for the world! Now,' she said, changing the subject suddenly. 'I simply must have you meet Angela, my long-lost cousin!'

'We have already met,' I said.

'Really? When was that? Angela darling,' she called, raising her voice. 'Do come and talk to us over here. I'm ready to share Charles with everyone else now.'

Angela Marchmont glided over from where she had been talking to Joan Havelock and greeted me with every appearance of pleasure. She was dressed in the same shimmering hues as when I had last met her, which brought to mind a graceful mermaid or similar mythical creature.

'How kind of you to take an interest in Joan,' said Rosamund. 'Although I love her dearly, she can be such an awkward girl at times. Whenever we have guests I am constantly on tenterhooks, terrified that she will frighten them all off by saying something dreadfully blunt about Major Lyttelton's carbuncle, or Lady Benlowes's snaggle teeth and then what will we do for company at weekends? The three of us will end up spending every evening staring across the table at each other like fish and asking each other to pass the salt and it will be too utterly dull for words.'

We laughed at Rosamund's comically mournful look.

'I think you're exaggerating a little, Rosamund dear,' said Mrs. Marchmont. 'Joan is a charming girl; she is just at the shy, awkward stage, that's all. And she is making a great effort this evening, I'm sure to please you and Neville.' Indeed, when I looked across the room, Joan Havelock was laughing merrily as she listened to Bobs telling one of his tall tales, while Simon Gale stood by silently.

'Well, I shall go and do my duty and encourage her,' replied Rosamund and moved across to the little group.

I fell into conversation with Angela Marchmont. She was very easy to talk to and if the truth be told, her presence was something of a fresh breath of air, blowing away the grubbiness of the MacMurrays and the whirling sensation that Rosamund's appearance had caused in my head. We chatted about this and that and I was relieved to find that I was not expected to produce a lion's head from my pocket for her wall; nor did she ask me how much money I had made in South Africa, for which I was very grateful. I had begun to get the uncomfortable feeling that everybody present thought I was actually made of gold myself and half-expected that they would begin trying to snap bits off me to carry away. On returning to England after many years of moving in the most basic of societies, it had come as something of a shock to find out how engrossed by money all my acquaintances seemed to be. When I had left the country, talking about such things was considered dreadfully vulgar. No more, it appeared. I felt old-fashioned and out of step. I turned and found Mrs. Marchmont looking at me curiously. I could not help telling her a small part of what I had been thinking, although of course I did not refer directly to the company present. She nodded understandingly.

'Yes, I know what you mean,' she said. 'I felt exactly the same thing when I arrived in the States. There, everybody talks about money—how much they earn, how much their possessions cost, how much they expect to earn in future. It is considered quite normal and healthy and not at all vulgar. But they have a different way of looking at things over there.

In America, the view is that if one has worked very hard for years to make a success of things, then one has earned the right to display one's wealth and talk about it. The English have always had the opposite view—you know, the more one has, the less one ought to mention it—but I think it has become quite the fashion to copy the Americans. I am used to it now but you are more to be pitied, as you have only recently returned and it is all new to you.'

'It is,' I replied. 'And I don't think I quite like it.'

'But, you know, one could argue that there is at least no hypocrisy in talking about money. And why shouldn't one talk about it? We talk about the weather, politics, people we know. What is so different about money? After all, it is one of the most fundamental things in life.'

I thought for a moment.

'I see what you mean,' I said. 'But I don't think it's the money itself. It's the preoccupation with it. I was always taught not to bore people with my money concerns. We English have never liked people who boast about their wealth, or people who seem to be unduly concerned with having money above all else. We are supposed to enjoy our riches or suffer our poverty in a respectable silence. The Americans can do what they like but I think I prefer our way.'

Mrs. Marchmont laughed.

'Then I shall take good care not to seem too interested in money. If I accidentally drop a shilling out of my purse you must be sure not to mention it,' she said.

'Now you are teasing me. Was I being dreadfully pompous?'

'Not at all.'

'No, you're right, I was being pompous. I have no right to complain about these things.' It had in fact just struck me that I was possibly being a little hypocritical myself. Had I not spent the past few weeks ostentatiously dining at the Ritz and enjoying my new-found affluence in the flesh-pots of London? Perhaps I, too, had adopted the new attitude without realizing it.

The gong sounded and we all went off to dress, with the anxious encouragement of Sir Neville, who was a punctual sort. I was escorted up an imposing staircase and along a gal-leried landing and shown to a spacious room with a brightly -burning fire. I went to the window and pulled back the cur-tain but there was no moon and it was too dark to see very much. As I dressed, I reflected on the past hour or two. On the whole, I considered I had carried off the meeting with Rosamund rather well. How absurd of me, I thought, to be worried about making a fool of myself. Everything had been perfectly friendly and normal, with no awkward moments at all. On viewing my reflection in the glass, I found I was grinning idiotically and realized how much I must have been dreading the meeting. I felt as though a great weight had been lifted from me. Just then, a servant arrived.

'Her ladyship sent me to ask you if you have everything you require, sir,' she said.

'Thank her ladyship and tell her that nothing has been forgotten,' I said and she went off. I left the room and ran downstairs with a light heart. At the bottom of the stairs I was almost floored by one of the terriers, who darted out from a dark side-passage and skipped about under my feet ecstatically.

'Dodie! Get down!' barked Sir Neville, emerging from the passage with the other dog, as I hopped about and muttered imprecations under my breath. 'You must watch out for the dogs, Charles. Dodie in particular is a little devil. Just high spirits, that's all. They get very excited when we have visitors.'

'So I see!' I exclaimed. 'I shall have to be very careful then. I should hate to break any bones.'

Sir Neville gave a short guffaw.

'Come into my study,' he said. 'There's just time for a quick one before dinner.' He turned and led me back down the passage and into his study, which was comfortably furnished in a masculine style. I noticed that some of the furniture was rather worn. Some odd-looking wooden artefacts lay about on various shelves. I had seen many things of the sort while I was in Africa and felt a sudden pang of homesickness, which surprised me.

'I see you're admiring my native works of art,' said Sir Neville. 'I picked them up years ago on my travels. Most people think they're ugly but I like them. They remind me of my carefree youth.' He poured out two glasses of whisky from a decanter. 'As you can see, this is my place of refuge. Rosamund is dying to get in here and refurbish the place but I won't let her. I'm comfortable as I am, I tell her.' He handed me a glass. 'What do you think of this, then? I discovered it a couple of years ago. I get it from a chap I know in London— dreadful little oily-haired Cockney but he knows his stuff all right. I can give you his name if you like. Unless you're one of these modern young types who prefers cocktails.'

I duly expressed my appreciation of the whisky, which was indeed excellent and we sat in silence for a moment or two, as I gazed at one of the rough wooden figures and thought of the faraway land from whence it had come. Just then, a small noise attracted my attention and I looked up to find that Sir Neville was shifting about uncomfortably in his chair and clearing his throat. He obviously had something to say to me.

'Charles,' he began, then stopped and tugged his moustache. He coughed and tried again. 'So, what do you think of our little set-up here?'

I was almost certain that this was not the question he had intended to ask but I replied warmly, in praise of his house, his grounds, his wife and his comfortable domestic arrangements. He smiled but I sensed he was distracted and had not actually heard what I said. There was a pause.

'You know, you are the very image of your father,' he said.

'So I have been told,' I replied.

'Terrible thing, the way it all ended,' he said gruffly. 'Terrible—terrible.'

I was silent. It was a period of my life which I preferred to forget.

'But you are not your father, of course. Your life has followed a very different pattern. You have been toughened up by hard work and the hot climate. Those are the things that really test the mettle and honesty of a man.'

I frowned. In spite of the views of the world at large, I still believed my father to have been a man of honour and any implication that he had been otherwise was still very painful to me, even though I had endured years of whispers and remarks on the subject.

'It is difficult,' continued Sir Neville, almost as though talking to himself. 'These things all seem to come at once. I have been most upset lately, most upset. Believe me, Charles, when I say there is nothing worse than finding out that you have been deceived in someone. But lately I have begun to feel that I am surrounded by liars and schemers.'

Was he talking about me? We were hardly close friends, so it seemed unlikely. My mind leapt involuntarily to the Mac-Murrays, who appeared, even on my short acquaintance, potentially to fit the description. Was he referring to them? In that case, why speak to me about it?

'What do you mean?' I asked.

At the sound of my words, he seemed to emerge from his reverie.

'I beg your pardon, Charles. Do forgive my ramblings. I am old-fashioned and have never been able to accustom myself to the modern ways and manners. Rosamund is always telling me that I am stuck in the past and I dare say she's right. Now, about these prospecting rights.' Sir Neville began rummaging through some papers in his desk drawer. 'I have something to show you that may surprise you. Indeed it surprised me very much, and I should like to know what you have to say about it as I hardly know whether to believe it.'

We moved on to other topics.

A few minutes afterwards the bell rang, summoning us to dinner, for which I was rather thankful. As I followed Sir

Neville along the passage towards the hall, I thought back to our conversation. As far as I had been able to judge in the short time I had been in the house, everybody seemed to be on perfectly amicable and easy terms and yet Sir Neville had spoken of liars and schemers. Whom could he have been referring to?

CHAPTER FIVE

THE DINING-ROOM was a rather grand affair, with panelled walls and rich damask curtains. I was seated between Rosamund and Gwen MacMurray—a ticklish prospect that required all my powers of concentration, especially since it became evident as early as the soup course that Gwen was determined that I should devote all my attention to her rather than Rosamund and Rosamund was equally determined that I should devote all my attention to *her*. Bobs, meanwhile, sat opposite, with a perfectly straight face, belied by a wicked gleam in his eye and did his best to stir things up as much as possible. By the time the fish arrived, the two ladies were becoming quite heated and Bobs was struggling to maintain his composure, but fortunately we were all rescued by Angela Marchmont, who addressed a question about something or other to Gwen from the other end of the table which demanded a long reply. Disaster was averted and Rosamund stood triumphant.

I complimented her on the dinner and the smooth running of her household.

'Yes,' she sighed. 'But it is a permanent struggle to keep things in order. 'Sissingham is so remote that it is difficult to keep hold of good servants. These days all the girls want to work in the towns and I have to pay a simply enormous wage to the cook and the housekeeper, who were originally at the London house. But I can't do without either of them, so I stump up willingly.'

'And so you ought,' said Bobs. 'It must be terribly dull for a girl stuck here miles from anywhere, especially on her day off, when she would rather be out dancing with her young man.'

'Yes,' said Rosamund.

'Still, perhaps one day you will move back to London, then you will be able to find as many good servants as your little heart desires and all your maids will be able to go out dancing as often as they want.'

'And when will that be?' asked Rosamund slowly. There was an odd expression on her face that I did not quite understand.

'As soon as you like,' said Bobs. 'You better than anyone know how to square things with Neville. All you have to do is say the word and you can be back where you belong in less than no time!'

'If only it were that easy.'

'But of course it is! A wife always knows the best way to get round her husband whenever she wants something. And I'm quite sure you are no exception.'

'I have asked him. You know I have. Lots of times. He always says "not yet".'

'You dreadful old plotter, Bobs,' I said. 'I really do believe you enjoy causing strife wherever you go.'

'Oh, he does! Isn't he awful?' cried Rosamund. 'And after all the effort I went to earlier to convince you that I would quite happily stay at Sissingham for the rest of my days! Charles, what I said before was absolutely true but you know Bobs as well as I do—he is a dreadful tempter into mischief. Sometimes I think he is actually in league with the devil. Get thee behind me, Bobs!' she commanded, mockingly.

'Nonsense,' said Bobs. 'I am simply saying that if you want something, then you must do everything in your power to get it.'

'But what if somebody else doesn't want me to have it?'

'There are ways,' replied Bobs, mysteriously.

'I agree with Bobs,' said Gwen, who had caught the last part of our conversation. 'When I know what I want, I never let anyone stop me from getting it.'

'Careful, that's dangerous talk,' said Bobs.

'But it's true,' she insisted. 'I'm very good at getting my own way. When I met Hugh, for example, he was all but engaged to someone else but I got him to break it off.'

'Oh indeed? I should be most interested to hear exactly how you did that,' said Bobs. The words in themselves were innocent enough but there was meaning in his tone.

Gwen opened her mouth to continue, then went slightly pink.

'You horrid thing!' she exclaimed, tossing her head. 'I shan't tell you anything about it now.'

She turned away and Bobs smirked.

'Bobs, I will not have you being disrespectful to my guests,' murmured Rosamund but without a great deal of conviction.

'You're right,' said Bobs. 'Gwen, please forgive me. I am an incorrigible tease and deserve to be roasted over hot coals for eternity.'

'Oh, very well then,' said Gwen, slightly mollified.

'But I warn you now, I shall continue to tease you whenever the opportunity presents itself.'

'That goes without saying,' I said.

More serious subjects were under discussion at the other end of the table, where everyone was talking about the latest details of a sensational trial that had been the biggest story in the newspapers in recent weeks. The accused was a woman who was supposed to have killed her elderly mother with a poker in a sudden fit of rage. It was a sordid story, which had for some reason captured the imagination of the public.

'I don't care how ghastly the old woman was,' Hugh Mac-Murray said. 'I don't believe any woman would brain her mother with a fire-iron. It's unnatural. I could believe it if she had poisoned her but physical violence is not a woman's crime.'

'You can never tell, though. Some people are very good at repressing their real characters, sometimes even for years,' said Joan. 'It's all to do with psychology, or something. There was a girl at school like that. She seemed perfectly normal, except that you never knew what she was thinking. Then one day she found that her bicycle had a puncture when she needed it in a hurry and flew into a terrible rage. She started kicking it and shouting at it. She kicked it and kicked it until she bent the wheel out of shape, while the girls all stared at her in astonishment. Then she ran upstairs and came into the common-room an hour later as though nothing had happened. Nobody knew what to say to her after that but we all took care not to do anything to offend her!'

Everyone laughed but I noticed that Simon Gale was looking rather white. With his delicate constitution, perhaps he found all this talk of violence upsetting.

We did not sit long at the table after the ladies had retired and when we returned to the drawing-room we found them laughing and congregated around the gramophone. We were all feeling rather gay and one or two couples soon started dancing. Sir Neville stood it as long as he could but then excused himself, saying that he had some urgent papers to work on. He appeared to have lapsed into gloom once again.

'Do you require my assistance, Sir Neville?' asked Simon Gale.

'No, no, Gale, that's quite all right. The ladies need your services here, for the dancing.' He nodded round at everyone and left the room.

'I say, what's the matter with old Neville?' said Bobs but nobody replied.

'Come and dance with me,' said Sylvia to me, as another song began.

'As you wish, my lady,' I replied with a bow and she pulled me towards the gramophone. She moved gracefully and as we danced I thought how pretty she looked in the evening glow.

'I know one shouldn't ask—' she said, then paused uncertainly. I smiled. I had no doubt what was on her mind.

'What shouldn't one ask?'

'Well, I just was just wondering—about earlier this evening and you and Rosamund.'

'What about me and Rosamund?'

'Drat you, Charles, you know exactly what I mean!'

'I think you are a very curious young lady,' I remarked.

'Oh, I am!' she exclaimed. 'Isn't it awful? I was simply dying to hear what you and Rosamund were talking about but Hugh got hold of me and started telling me some interminable story and I was forced to listen. But now you must tell me—what was it like, meeting her again after all this time? Don't say you felt nothing, because I shan't believe you.'

I looked at her eager, anxious face, then threw back my head and laughed.

'You little minx! I've a good mind to take you to task for your impertinence. But, to reply to your question, yes, of course I felt something. I felt delighted to meet Rosamund again as an old friend. There! Does that satisfy you?'

'Not exactly but I suppose it's too much to expect you to be indiscreet. Drat Hugh and his stories!'

'There's nothing to be indiscreet about. We chatted about what we had both been doing for the past eight years, that is all,' I said.

'I see,' she said. The music ended and we moved over to the recessed window. Sylvia peered out into the gloom and then turned to me. I lit cigarettes for us both.

'How do you like my frock?' she asked abruptly. 'I bought it especially for this weekend but you have never mentioned it.'

'It's very pretty,' I replied, in some amusement at her bluntness. She gave a wide smile.

'But of course, you have to say that, now that I've asked you. You know, Charles, you are not exactly a gentleman. A woman should not have to elicit compliments from a man.'

'I thought girls didn't care about that sort of thing nowadays.'

'Of course we do! Why does one buy a new dress if not to be noticed?'

'I'm afraid I have always been rather tongue-tied when it comes to saying the right things to women. Bobs was always better at it than I.'

'Nonsense! Don't tell me that all those years abroad have made you forget how to behave in the company of women. I have been watching you this evening and I simply don't believe it.'

'Oh, you have been watching me, have you? For what purpose?'

She blushed slightly.

'I don't mean watching you, exactly. Keeping an eye out, perhaps. I am a little concerned about you.'

'What on earth for?' I asked, surprised.

'Well, you have been away for so long and things have changed in that time, in ways of which you might not be aware.'

'I don't think I quite understand you.'

'It's difficult to explain. How can I put it? I meant that while you have been away, the people you left behind have carried on with their lives and have done things and said things and thought things in your absence. And everything that a person does, or says, or thinks, causes that person to change— even if it's just a little bit at a time. And then after many years, all those little changes can add up to a big change. So you see, now that you have returned, you could find that you are talking to someone, thinking that they are the same person as they were eight years ago, whereas in fact they are someone quite different.'

'You mean you are worried that I will go blundering about and saying the wrong things to the wrong people?' I was a little offended at the suggestion.

'No, of course I didn't mean anything like that. It's just that you are terribly upright and honest and I should hate for you to return to England only to be disillusioned and leave again.'

'What has my uprightness and honesty to do with anything?'

'There! Now you are cross,' said Sylvia. 'I told you I should never make a diplomat's wife. I try to say nice things to people but they always come out wrong.'

'Don't be silly. Of course I'm not cross,' I said. 'It is kind of you to be concerned about me but I can I assure you it's quite unnecessary.'

'What are you two talking about so confidentially behind the curtain there?' demanded Rosamund from across the room. 'Sylvia, would you be a darling and help make up a four?'

I held the curtain aside to let Sylvia pass into the room and join Rosamund, Hugh MacMurray and Simon Gale, who were preparing to play.

'Come and shake a leg, Gwen,' said Bobs, busy at the gramophone. 'Just to show there are no hard feelings.'

'What an extraordinary expression,' said Gwen but stood up without apparent reluctance. As always, I felt a sense of wonder, tinged with a certain amount of envy, at Bobs's ability to charm everyone he met. He had involved himself in some fairly outrageous escapades over the years—I, who had known him from childhood, knew that only too well and had often been called upon to extricate him from some scrape or other—but he never seemed to get into serious trouble over them. Instead, he would disarm the offended party with a rueful apology and a schoolboyish wrinkle of the nose and once forgiven, would often go on immediately to do something even more dreadful. Thinking back to some of his adventures in particular, I was certain that had I done some of the things Bobs had been guilty of, I would have been ostracized by everyone I knew.

Angela Marchmont was sitting alone, watching Bobs and Gwen indulgently. I moved over to join her.

'I do hope you haven't come to ask me to dance,' she said. 'I have already danced once with Bobs and he whirled me round so vigorously I feared bones would be broken—my own in particular!'

'Don't worry,' I said. 'I think I should make a poor showing against Bobs anyhow. He is well-known around London for his energetic dancing. I understand he regularly receives bills from night-clubs for broken furniture.'

'I can well believe it!' she replied.

I was curious to know more about her relationship with Rosamund.

'It must seem strange, having to become acquainted with your cousin all over again after all these years,' I said.

'It was at first, certainly. I am about ten years older than she is, you know and she was still quite a child when I left England, so when we met again in August it was rather odd, seeing her for the first time as an adult. However, we had written to each other often over the years, so it was not quite as difficult as one might expect.'

'Did you find that she had changed at all? Her personality, I mean?'

'In some respects, perhaps. We all change to a certain extent as we grow older—it is to be hoped for the better. In other respects, though, she was exactly the little girl I had left behind.'

'The same wilfulness?'

'That, certainly,' laughed Angela.

'What are you two laughing about over there?' demanded Rosamund, looking up from her cards.

'We were talking about you, darling,' said Angela.

'How lovely! I like people to talk about me—as long as they say nice things, of course. I hope you were telling each other how delightful I am.'

'But of course,' I said.

Rosamund turned back to the game and Angela and I resumed our conversation. After a few minutes, Joan Havelock, who had been reading alone in a far corner, yawned, closed her book with a snap and wandered over to join us.

'How terribly tired I am!' she said. 'Mr. Knox, you will think I am dreadful for saying this but I find company exhausting, much as I enjoy it. I'm sure one uses up more energy in smiling than in frowning and one has to smile all the time when one has guests!'

'That may be the case but it is certainly worth the effort,' said Angela. 'Firstly, it keeps your guests happy and secondly, you look so much prettier when you smile!'

'You always know the right thing to say,' said Joan affectionately. 'I wish I did. I'm afraid I shall never be a grand society hostess like Rosamund, however.'

My mind went back to my earlier conversation with Rosamund. The uncomfortable truth was that Rosamund was not, after all, a grand society hostess. Here she was, buried in deepest Norfolk with an elderly husband and with only local dignitaries—and such of her friends who were prepared to make the journey—to entertain. She had said she was happy but could that really be true?

CHAPTER SIX

O N GOING DOWNSTAIRS the next morning I found the other members of the house party sitting around the breakfast table in listless mood after the gaiety of the night before, a mood which I attributed partly to the rain pattering against the window. It seemed as though it had settled in solidly for the rest of the day and we spent the morning scattered about in various rooms of the house, each engaged in our own business. Sir Neville and Simon Gale went off to the study, while Mrs. Marchmont disappeared to write some letters and make a telephone-call. I soon recollected that I had one or two letters to write myself and returned to my room as soon as the maids had finished.

By lunch-time, however, the weather appeared to have cleared. It had stopped raining at least and there were signs that the clouds were thinning, and when I joined the others at the table I found that the mood had lifted somewhat. At luncheon, we learned that we were expecting a visitor in the shape of Sir Neville's solicitor, Mr. Pomfrey. He was coming to look over some papers with Sir Neville but would be a guest that evening for dinner.

'Changing the old last will and testament, Neville, is that it?' said Bobs. 'I say, the rest of you had better look out and be especially polite to him today, or you might find yourselves disinherited. Have any of you offended him lately?'

I glanced around but only one or two people laughed in response to this pleasantry. Gwen MacMurray in particular looked as though she did not find it at all amusing. Evidently the shaft had hit rather closer to home than Bobs had intended. Sir Neville coughed.

'Mr. Pomfrey is an old family friend and often visits us here,' he said. 'In fact, I believe you have met him before, Bobs.'

'Yes,' said Rosamund. 'He was here only a month or two ago. You must remember that weekend, Bobs.'

'Oh yes, I remember him all right,' said Bobs. 'About five feet tall and one hundred and six years old. He looked as though he would blow away at the first gust of wind but when he shook my hand he nearly crushed all the bones in it. Gave me quite a shock, I can tell you.'

'He is a bit of a dry old stick,' agreed Joan. 'But he's all right. He has always been very kind to me. He knows an awful lot about gardening. I wanted to ask him about his roses.'

'Well, he will be here at four, so you can ask him then,' said Rosamund. The talk moved on to other subjects and it was only later that I realized that Sir Neville had not actually denied the accusation that he was planning to change his will. I supposed, however, that he had seen no need to reply to what was just another one of Bobs's rather tasteless jokes.

By two o'clock, the weather had cleared completely and I took a turn in the garden with Joan Havelock and the two dogs, who raced off excitedly. Joan was in talkative mood.

'I hope things aren't too deadly dull for you here,' she said. 'It's rather a small party, I'm afraid. Rosamund did invite some other friends of hers but they couldn't come. And Neville is not himself. He has been more or less down in the dumps all week, I don't know why. Of course, Bobs and Sylvia are always great fun. They come here very often, you know.'

I hastened to assure her that I was by no means bored.

'Good. I am pleased,' she said. 'I know Rosamund was anxious that you should not find us too stuck in the mud out here. To tell the truth, she was rather cross that she couldn't muster a larger party. I think she wanted to impress you.'

'Really?'

'Of course. It's only natural, given what has passed between you. Didn't you want to impress *her*?'

I thought shame-facedly of the smart new clothes I had carefully packed and the neat hair-cut I had had before setting off for Norfolk and was silent. I found some of Joan's observations a little too uncomfortably accurate.

'What do you think of the MacMurrays?' was her next question.

I had no intention of telling her what I thought of the Mac-Murrays.

'They seem very pleasant people,' I replied.

Joan laughed.

'Oh, you needn't be tactful with me,' she said. 'I saw your face yesterday when Gwen got her hooks into you. You were a picture! But I quite agree with you,' she went on, answering my unspoken rather than my spoken comment, 'they are ghastly. Well, she is at any rate.' She then told me a scandalous rumour about Mrs. MacMurray which I shall not reproduce here. I was shocked and was about to reply stiffly, when we were joined by Angela Marchmont, who appeared just then around the corner of the house.

'Why, Mr. Knox,' she said. 'You look as though you had just had a fright!'

'Oh, I was telling him that old story about Gwen. I think I must have shocked him.'

'If it is the one I think you mean, Joan darling, I don't think you are being quite fair to Gwen to be repeating such a tale, which is not very nice and is probably not true. Nor is it fair to Mr. Knox, who is entitled to judge people on their own merits and not on what you tell him.'

It was all said very calmly and pleasantly. Joan looked a little sheepish.

'I suppose it isn't really the thing to go around telling stories that might not be true but it was Bobs who told me and he swore it was,' she said. 'And really, she is so exasperating. I don't know why we have to have them here so often. She always makes catty remarks about my figure and my clothes, all the while pretending to be as sweet as sugar. You know the kind of thing I mean: "You'd look simply marvellous in this dress, darling, if you just got rid of that little bit of extra weight on your hips and had better skin. It's exactly your colour".

Despite my disapproval, I smiled at her accurate mimicking of Gwen MacMurray.

Mrs. Marchmont laughed and excused herself, as she had only been passing that way in order to fetch a scarf from the house. We watched her as she moved off.

'I suppose I ought to be cross with Angela for giving me a ticking-off but I can't. She's such a dear,' said Joan.

In spite of myself, I was curious to know more about the MacMurrays and could not help saying so.

'I gather you are not fond of them,' I said.

Joan wrinkled her nose.

'Not particularly. Hugh is Neville's cousin, so they have a standing invitation to visit, pretty much. They're here practically all the time and seem to stay forever. Of course, it's only because they've got no money. But Hugh also wants to butter Neville up so as to make sure he gets pots of cash when Neville dies.'

'So he is mentioned in Sir Neville's will, then?'

'Oh yes. I think he comes into quite a lot of money. Didn't you see their faces at lunch, when Bobs made that joke about Neville's changing his will? They both looked like thunder. It would hit them hard if they had nothing to look forward to. Hugh was never very rich but now he has married Gwen he is even less so. You must have seen how expensively she dresses. They live a very fast life in town, too and mix with a rather disreputable crowd. Gwen in particular would simply tear her hair out if she hadn't Neville's money to look forward to. She maintains a decent pretence most of the time but when she has had too many cocktails she talks about it quite openly.'

Joan's information tallied perfectly with my own experiences and my own impressions of the MacMurrays.

'But you don't really think that Sir Neville is going to change his will, do you? Surely it was just a joke on Bobs's part.'

'I wouldn't be too sure of that,' replied Joan, lowering her voice, even though there was no-one around. 'In fact, if you'll promise not to tick me off again, I'll tell you something I heard yesterday.'

My good and bad selves struggled with each other briefly but my curiosity won the day.

'Go on,' I said.

'Well, I was in the library yesterday afternoon, looking for a book. I had the window open, as it was a nice afternoon and the place can get awfully musty. I wasn't thinking about anything in particular except my book but then I heard two people walking about on the terrace under the window. I didn't see either of them but one was Neville—I recognized his voice immediately. He seemed to be very angry about something, I don't know what exactly but then as they passed directly under the window, I heard him say, "Don't think you will be getting any money from me. That's all finished now", or something of the sort. I promise I wasn't eavesdropping— it all happened before I could move away.'

'How could you be sure it was MacMurray with him?' I asked.

'Who else could it have been? None of the other guests had arrived at that time.'

I had no answer to this.

'In any case, you don't seem to have heard very much of the conversation, so perhaps it was all something quite innocent,' I said. 'Perhaps Sir Neville was refusing to pay a dishonest tradesman or something of the kind.'

Joan snorted and looked disbelieving but was prevented from replying by the arrival of Simon Gale, who told us he was just going to fetch Mr. Pomfrey from the station. We watched him depart in the car and Joan said:

'Poor Simon! One can't help but feel sorry for him, working here.'

'He told me he was very happy here,' I said, surprised.

'Of course he did. He would hardly tell you otherwise, would he? But Neville works him very hard and Simon is really not up to it. He had a terrible War, you know and was ill for quite a long time afterwards. I don't think Neville means to treat Simon badly but he doesn't have much sympathy for sensitive people, especially men and I don't think he believes in shell shock.'

I had never been much of a believer in it myself but it seemed useless to argue, as I saw that Joan's sympathies were all with Gale, so I nodded understandingly.

We headed back towards the house and wandered slowly around the formal garden that lay behind it, then stopped for a moment by a ha-ha that bordered one of the lawns to look at the building, which appeared very handsome and stately in the late afternoon light. I lost myself in a day-dream for a few minutes, picturing myself and Sylvia in just such a house of our own, taking the dogs for a stroll around the grounds, she looking up at me and laughing at something terribly witty that I had just said, and then returning for tea in front of a roaring fire. It was an attractive picture and yet at the same time unconvincing. My day-dream held a shadow—of what I knew not; it was too blurred and indistinct—but there was *something* there that contrasted with the bright, cheerful picture in my head and made the whole image seem somehow artificial.

'Here are Rosamund and Bobs,' said Joan. 'I wonder what they've been doing.'

It was indeed Rosamund and Bobs, who had just come on to the lawn from the path that led round past the conservatory to the front of the house. They waved and we started forward to meet them.

'There you are!' said Rosamund. 'We were wondering what had happened to everybody. We haven't seen anyone for simply hours!'

'That's probably because you insisted we walk as far away from the house as possible, to the very furthest corner of the grounds,' said Bobs.

'Nonsense, I did no such thing!' exclaimed Rosamund. 'Do you like our park, Charles? Of course, the formal garden is simply ghastly but we shall be starting work on that in the spring. I thought we might have a small shrubbery instead.'

Perhaps it was that same afternoon light which had shown off the house to such flattering effect, or perhaps it was the health-giving exercise, but she looked absolutely radiant. Marriage to a wealthy man certainly suited Rosamund, as I had always suspected it would and for the first time since I had arrived, I was conscious of a regret that I had thought long since dead and buried.

'Joan, must you take those awful dogs everywhere with you? They do get under one's feet so and they're such a bore,' said Rosamund, as we entered the house through the conservatory.

'Don't be unfair, Rosamund,' said Joan reproachfully. 'They have never given you any trouble. It isn't you that looks after them, it's me or Neville and they only get under your feet if you don't look where you're going.'

'Rosamund demands that the path of life be smoothed for her without any effort on her part,' observed Bobs.

'Of course I do,' answered Rosamund, with disarming honesty. 'I should like to have everything fall into my lap. And why shouldn't I? There's no harm in it.'

Her remark brought to mind Gwen MacMurray, who had expressed a very similar sentiment the previous evening and I wondered how it was that a trait which struck me as so ugly in one woman could be so attractive in another.

We found the others gathered in the drawing-room for tea, together with a new member of the party, who I gathered must be Mr. Pomfrey. He was a dried-up little old fellow with, as Bobs had mentioned, a crushing hand-shake. He was evidently a great authority on gardening and Joan began questioning him closely about some new treatment for black fly she had heard of. As I sipped my tea, I noticed that Gwen MacMurray was eyeing Mr. Pomfrey with interest and I watched with amusement as she moved over to where he was standing and neatly cut Joan out. There was a low whistle next to me and I turned to find that Bobs had seen it too.

'As neat a job as I ever saw,' he said.

'Shh! She'll hear you.'

'What do you think? Is she pumping old Pomfrey for information? I'll bet she is simply dying to know why he's come here this afternoon. She's got the wind up her all right—terrified that she's not going to see a penny of Neville's money.'

'Is he really going to rewrite his will?' I asked. I had thought Bobs's remark at lunch-time was just a joke but Joan's story had given me pause for thought. Bobs shrugged his shoulders.

'No idea, although I shouldn't be surprised. Neville's rather a stuffy old fellow and I can't imagine him being too pleased if he knew what they get up to in town.'

I dismissed this reply as Bobs's usual rumour-mongering and concluded that Mr. Pomfrey was probably here for other reasons. It seemed unlikely that Sir Neville should advertise an intention to alter his will so openly, especially when the people who would be most affected by the change were actually in the house. I glanced over at Hugh MacMurray, who was looking as cheerful as ever, seemingly oblivious to rumours about his supposed impending impoverishment. He was roaring with laughter at something Angela Marchmont was saying and seemed to have not a care in the world.

Gwen at last released the solicitor from her clutches and I heard Sir Neville say: 'Shall we return to the study, Pomfrey? There are just a few more points I should like to mention.'

'Certainly,' replied Mr. Pomfrey. 'Indeed, as I said before, the course you wish to take carries certain...implications, shall we say? I am convinced we ought to discuss these more at length before I carry out the actions you mentioned.'

He excused himself to the company at large and they left the room together. I looked over at Gwen MacMurray, to see if I could judge whether or not she had had any success in finding out the purpose of Mr. Pomfrey's visit but her face gave nothing away.

That night, at dinner, I was seated next to the solicitor and found him to be a likeable little fellow, intelligent with a dry sense of humour. He had obviously mixed a good deal in society and had a fund of mildly indiscreet anecdotes with which he entertained Angela Marchmont (who was sitting on the other side of him) and me throughout dinner while the rest of the table shrieked and laughed uproariously at some of Bobs's past escapades, which he was recounting with great relish.

'We were all talking last night about the Mason case,' I said, 'and between us were unable to agree on whether or not the accused is guilty.'

'Much like the rest of England, I imagine,' replied Mr. Pomfrey. 'Did you reach a conclusion?'

'Not at all. There was much debate about whether the crime was "in character", so to speak. Some found it difficult to believe that a woman could have committed the murder at all. We tend to think of violence as being the preserve of men and although we all know that there have been many women murderers, they generally use more subtle weapons, such as poison. All the neighbours said that Aline Mason was a delightful girl. Somebody else must have done it, surely?'

'It might seem so,' he replied cautiously. 'And yet, I myself can think of several examples in which a woman of apparently calm temper has resorted to violence.'

'Yes, Joan was telling us of a school-mate of hers who did that,' said Angela, who had been on the side of the 'possibles'. 'And I myself witnessed something of a similar nature, years ago, although in this case it was an instance of a child that lost its temper unexpectedly and beat a dog so savagely that it had to be destroyed.'

'Indeed? Where was that?'

'Oh, it was several years ago, in—in New York. The child belonged to some friends and had always been believed to have a particularly sunny nature.' She looked as though she wished to say more but thought better of it.

'What an odious child! I hope he was severely chastised,' I said. 'What became of him? Did he grow up to be a useful member of society?'

'I believe so,' said Angela, smiling.

'Well, it just shows that you can never tell,' said Mr. Pomfrey. 'For myself, I am inclined to believe that Miss Mason did in fact kill her mother, although we may never find out the real truth. Juries often have a lot of sympathy for pretty young women who stand before them in the dock.'

'Yes,' said Angela. She looked thoughtful but said no more.

The ladies soon retired and when we joined them, Sir Neville again stayed for only a short while before withdrawing to his study. This time, his departure caused no remark but I could not help thinking again about the conversation we had had the night before and wondering what he had meant when he had talked of 'liars and schemers'.

Once again, the gramophone was put to use, although nobody seemed to be in the mood for dancing. For some reason that I could not quite put my finger on, the atmosphere was one of general awkwardness: whereas last night we had all been very gay, tonight everyone seemed rather tetchy and gloomy. Various people wandered in and out of the room without making much effort to join in the conversation. Joan and Gwen had descended into a state of barely-concealed mutual hostility, while Bobs's occasional attempts at jokes all fell flat and Sylvia sat in silence by the window. Only Angela and Mr. Pomfrey seemed unaffected; they sat together at one end of the room and chatted merrily.

'Darlings, no wonder you're all sitting there like the end of the world. This song is simply too dreary!' exclaimed Rosamund, hurrying breathlessly into the room. She looked through the gramophone records and selected a much livelier air. 'There! Now, which of you men would like to dance with me? Mr. Pomfrey, I know you won't refuse!'

Mr. Pomfrey gave a dry chuckle.

'My dear Lady Strickland, I applaud your optimism but I fear the speed of this modern music would be quite too much for me. Perhaps Mr. Buckley will oblige instead for this song. However, if later on you should decide to play something more appropriate to my advanced age and declining energy, I assure you I shall be most honoured!'

Bobs, as ever, was happy to oblige but despite the change of music, there still seemed to be something wrong with us all. I wondered what it was and could only suppose at last that it had something to do with the arrival of the solicitor—or rather, what he potentially represented, since he himself was perfectly inoffensive.

When the song had finished, a slower one was found and Rosamund insisted that Mr. Pomfrey keep his promise, which he did with great solemnity. Ever the perfect hostess, she seemed determined that we should all be happy. She danced with all the men in turn, though none of the other women showed an inclination to join in and kept up a constant flow of gay chatter, first with one of us, then another. I admired her activity enormously and was surprised and pleased to find that her efforts were proving successful, as the atmosphere began to lighten perceptibly. Having danced until she was breathless, she then coaxed us into playing a game of Consequences, which had us all roaring with laughter by the end.

'Oh!' said Rosamund, wiping her eyes after one particularly silly round. 'I must remember to play this game the next time my guests are bored and threatening to leave! I declare I haven't played this since I was a child but I am glad I remembered it.'

'Perhaps we can get Neville to come and play,' suggested Joan. 'It might cheer him up a bit.'

'What a good idea!' said Rosamund, after a pause. 'Charles, you shall come with me and help me persuade him. He may be grumpy with me but he can't say no to a guest, can he?'

She pulled me out of the room before I could protest and ran lightly ahead of me along to the study.

'Bother! Why on earth has he locked the door?' she said. She knocked and listened.

'Darling, do leave those fusty old papers and come along to the drawing-room,' she said loudly. She grimaced and shook her head at me as I approached. 'Are you sure?' she called. 'Well, then, don't stay up too late.'

She turned to me with a rueful look and we returned along the passage to the hall. 'I don't know what's the matter with him this week,' she said. 'It's really too bad of him to desert his guests but I can't do a thing with him when he is in this mood.'

We were met in the hall by Hugh MacMurray, who had just come in through a side door.

'Hallo!' said Rosamund. 'We've just been trying to persuade Neville to come and join us but he refused, didn't he, Charles?'

'Yes,' I agreed.

'Old Neville being stubborn, what?' said MacMurray. 'That's a shame. We shall all have to cheer him up. Brrr!' he continued, with a shiver. 'It's jolly cold out there! I shall need a stiff drink to warm myself.'

'Good gracious! Whatever possessed you to go outside at this time of the evening?' said Rosamund.

'Oh, I just wanted a breath of fresh air, you know. It was getting rather stuffy in the drawing-room,' he replied. I thought he looked a little sheepish.

'Any luck?' asked Joan as we returned to the drawing-room.

'None at all. He insists on remaining buried in his papers. Well, we shall just have to continue our fun without him.'

But it looked as though the lightening of mood had been only temporary. Nobody wanted to play another game of Consequences and Rosamund proposed cards in vain. Joan went out and came back with a book, while Simon Gale went off, murmuring about some work that he needed to finish and Bobs disappeared on mysterious business of his own.

'I want some more music!' said Gwen, a little too loudly. She had been drinking steadily all evening and was now swaying with great concentration over to the gramophone.

'Must we?' said Joan. 'I've a splitting headache.'

'What headache? You never mentioned it when we were playing the music before,' said Gwen.

'I didn't have it before. It only came on a few minutes ago.'

'How very convenient,' said Gwen. There was a dangerous edge to her voice which sounded a warning note.

'What do you mean?'

'I don't believe you have a headache at all—you just want to spoil the evening for everybody.'

Joan flared up at once.

'What rot! If anybody is spoiling the evening, it's you.'

'No it's not!'

'Yes it is! You always have to be the centre of attention. We were sitting here perfectly quietly but you had to disturb everything, just as you always do.'

'Darlings,' cried Rosamund, 'now do behave nicely. I hate to see you fall out when things were going so well.'

Gwen paid no attention but drew herself up indignantly.

'What do you mean, "just as I always do"? You beastly thing! Don't think I don't know your real opinion of me—I know you look down on us. You think we're not good enough to come here, it's perfectly obvious. You may think I don't notice your sneers every time we come here but I do. I see you trying to influence Neville against us!'

'I say old girl, look here,' began Hugh MacMurray, shifting uncomfortably.

'Be quiet, Hugh! I'm sick and tired of being insulted by these people. Don't you see they think you have married beneath you? No, of course, you have never noticed it—why should you? You don't have to put up with the whispers and the rumours and—and the people looking down their noses at you. If you were a real man you would defend me against them but you never do.'

Her husband emitted an unhappy bleating noise.

'And you are a fine one to make judgments!' Gwen continued to Joan. 'I've seen you mooning about after Simon like a love-struck cow, don't think I haven't. But really,' she burst into peals of laughter, 'who on earth would look twice at a great lump like you?'

There was a startled silence, then Joan burst into tears and hurried out of the room. Gwen appeared to have exhausted her ire. She sat down suddenly.

'I feel sick,' she announced dolefully. 'Boopsie, take me up to bed.'

Rosamund nodded to Hugh.

'Yes, dear,' he said and led her out of the room.

There was a general clearing of throats and somebody attempted to begin a conversation about the weather. Rosamund sat with her hand to her forehead for a moment and then heaved a great sigh.

'What a difficult evening this is! I think I shall just give up trying to make it a success and suggest that you all go to bed immediately. Why won't people behave as they are supposed to when I am trying to throw an elegant house party?'

'It is getting late. Perhaps we shall all feel better tomorrow after a good night's sleep,' said Angela.

I glanced at my watch and discovered that it was nearly half-past eleven. I was in fact rather tired myself but felt it would look cowardly if I were the first to leave. Fortunately, Mr. Pomfrey expressed his intention to retire immediately and was soon followed by Rosamund and Angela. I excused myself shortly afterwards and headed to my room, where I got into bed and lay awake for some time, before falling into an uncomfortable sleep.

CHAPTER SEVEN

I WAS WOKEN the next morning by the sound of running feet, followed by a general commotion that seemed to be coming from the direction of the stairs. Through a haze of sleep I peered at the clock and found that it was still early, turned over and attempted to drop off again. But the noise and bustle were insistent and seemed to be getting louder, so I reluctantly emerged from my comfortable bed, dressed and came downstairs. In the hall I found myself confronted by a scene of confusion. Half the servants seemed to be rushing about in varying degrees of uproar, while the old butler vainly tried to shoo them back to their quarters and a housemaid wailed loudly in the corner. I spotted Simon Gale and Mr. Pomfrey standing together in close consultation and joined them.

'Hallo, what the devil is going on here?' I asked.

'Mr. Knox, I am sorry to have to tell you that Sir Neville has met with an accident,' replied Mr. Pomfrey gravely. Simon Gale nodded. He was very white.

'What do you mean, an accident?' I demanded, looking from one to the other. 'Surely you don't mean he's—'

Mr. Pomfrey bowed his head.

'I am very much afraid that he is dead.'

I was bewildered.

'But how? What happened?'

'It—er—appears that he fell and hit his head on the mantelpiece some time last night. He was found this morning in his study.'

'Fell and hit his head?' I repeated stupidly. 'That seems very odd. How on earth did he do that?'

Simon Gale spoke, reluctantly it seemed.

'We are not quite certain of the exact sequence of events. All we know at present is that the housemaid who came down to clean the study this morning found the door locked. After a search, a spare key was eventually found by the butler and he and the housemaid entered the room to find Sir Neville lying by the fireplace, having apparently fallen. There was a glass lying on the floor next to him and a strong odour of whisky. Of course, there is no suggestion that he was at all inebriated,' he continued hastily.

'No, no, of course not,' said Mr. Pomfrey. 'But even taking a small amount may well have caused him to lose his balance more easily.'

'Rosamund—what about Rosamund?' I said suddenly. 'Has she been told?'

'Lady Strickland was informed shortly after the discovery was made,' replied the solicitor. 'She insisted on seeing Sir Neville alone. I did not think it right but she would not be dissuaded.' He shook his head. 'She is in the morning-room now with Miss Havelock and Mr. Buckley.'

'The doctor is on his way and should arrive shortly,' said Gale, 'although there is nothing to be done, I fear.' He swallowed. It looked rather as though he needed a strong whisky himself. 'Lady Strickland wanted Sir Neville to be carried to his room but Mr. Pomfrey quite rightly said that he must not be moved until the doctor has examined him.'

'Oh, quite so, quite so,' said the solicitor. 'The facts of the matter must be established, however distressing to the family. I have taken the precaution of locking the door again, in order to prevent curious servants from entering the room.'

He did not add: 'And curious guests' but the phrase hung in the air, unspoken.

The news had quite taken my breath away. I turned from the two men and entered the morning-room. Rosamund was seated on a low divan next to Joan, who was sobbing quietly into a handkerchief. Bobs was staring thoughtfully out of the window, with his hands in his pockets. Rosamund herself was white but quite composed. She looked up as I entered.

'Oh Charles!' she cried piteously. 'Whatever shall I do?'

I went over to her and took her hand but could find no words.

Bobs turned and saw me.

'Hallo, old thing,' he said, without a trace of his usual jocular manner. He looked rather shaken. 'Ghastly business, this, what?'

'When will the doctor come?' asked Rosamund. 'I want him to come now. I can't bear all this waiting.'

'He is on his way and will be here soon,' I said.

'He must come quickly, he must. Where is everybody else?'

'I've no idea. I assume they are all still asleep,' I replied.

'Perhaps that's best for the moment,' she said. 'I can't think what to do. What *does* one do in this situation?' She pressed her hands to her temples. 'I simply must *think* but my head is going round and round and I can't.'

'Hush,' I said. 'Don't try to think for the moment. There's no need, at least not until the doctor arrives.'

She gave an odd sort of smile.

'Dear Charles! Always so beautifully uncomplicated.' She looked about her in an agitated fashion. 'Where is Angela? I want Angela. She will look after me. Please, somebody, fetch Angela.'

'Here I am darling,' said Mrs. Marchmont, entering the room at that moment. She came over to where Rosamund was sitting and kissed her. 'I've just heard the news. My dear, I am so terribly sorry.' She straightened up and looked around at us all. 'The doctor has arrived and is now in the study.'

'Oh!' cried Rosamund, jumping up. 'At last! I must see him now.'

Before we could dissuade her, she hurried out of the room, followed by her cousin.

Sylvia arrived, looking white and breathless.

'Is it true?' she demanded. Nobody replied but one look at our faces was enough to tell her the truth.

Joan, perhaps mindful of her duties, made a visible effort to pull herself together and stood up, red-eyed.

'Well, there's no use in our sitting here all day and we can't be of any help now that the doctor and Mr. Pomfrey have taken charge. I think perhaps we should go in to breakfast,' she said, 'although I'm sure I shan't be able to eat a bite.'

We all trooped through to the dining-room in a dazed fashion and made a sketchy breakfast, attended by Rogers, the old butler, whose mind was clearly elsewhere. Afterwards, we all gathered in a huddle in the drawing-room, talking in hushed voices. It seemed as though we were all waiting for something, although I hardly knew what.

In the late morning, the MacMurrays finally descended and burst in upon us in a great hurry, having evidently just been informed of the tragedy.

'I say!' said MacMurray. 'What's all this about Neville? Surely it can't be true.' He looked appalled.

'I'm afraid it is,' I said.

He swung round to stare at me.

'Where did it happen?' he demanded.

'In his study. It must have been some time late last night.'

'Are you sure? But that's impossible!' he said. He sat down suddenly and put his head in his hands. 'Oh Lord,' he said. 'I need a drink.' He looked ghastly.

Gwen, if possible, looked even worse, although I thought some of that must be attributed to the amount she had drunk the previous evening. Her face was all blotched and puffy and her eyes darted this way and that as though she did not know quite where she was.

'What are we supposed to do now?' she asked.

'Wait here until the doctor has finished, I imagine,' I replied.

The rest of the morning seemed to drag on interminably. I felt that I ought to leave, an intruder in a tragedy that was not my own and yet at the same time I did not wish to appear as though I were deserting the family in its time of need. No-one else seemed to have any intention of going but of course they were all close friends or relations of Sir Neville, whereas I was a comparative stranger. I therefore sat uncomfortably, waiting uselessly for some indication of what I should do.

It was not until we had all gone into lunch that Mr. Pomfrey returned, accompanied by Angela Marchmont. The solicitor looked round at the questioning eyes that were raised to his from the table.

'Dr. Carter has finished examining Sir Neville,' he said. 'He is now with Lady Strickland, who has been persuaded to lie down for a few hours.'

'What did he say?' asked Joan.

'He appears to agree with our view that it was a tragic accident. Sir Neville was found lying next to the fireplace and it looks rather as though he lost his balance and fell backwards, hitting the back of his head on the edge of the mantelpiece as he did so. It may be of some comfort to you to know that death would have been almost instantaneous.'

'Where is poor Neville? Surely you haven't left him in the study?'

'Sir Neville has been carried to his room for now, until he can be—er—removed.'

'Where are the dogs?' said Joan, suddenly. 'Poor things. They won't have had their walk this morning. I'll take them out now. The fresh air will clear my head.' She rose from the table and went out.

'I think I shall take a walk too,' I said.

'I'll come with you,' said Sylvia.

We fetched our coats and went out through the side door. It was a dull day but the chill air was a welcome change from the oppressive atmosphere that prevailed in the house. We walked slowly up and down the terrace, deep in our own thoughts.

'It doesn't seem real, somehow,' Sylvia said eventually.

'No,' I agreed.

'How quickly one forgets about death,' she went on, almost as though talking to herself. 'I mean, it's only about ten years since Ralph died. I was just a kid then, of course. It's perfectly horrid but one picks oneself up and carries on, doesn't one?'

'I suppose one does,' I replied, thinking about my own parents' deaths.

'I hope Rosamund will be all right. I'd like to do something but one feels so desperately helpless. There is nothing one *can* do in such a situation as this—except perhaps be as unobtrusive as possible.'

'Yes—it must be especially difficult, having guests at a time like this. I shall offer my services of course but if they are declined I think the best thing I can do is to make as discreet and diplomatic an exit as possible.'

Just then, there was a rattle behind us and we turned to find that we were standing outside the French windows to the study.

'Hallo,' said Angela Marchmont, stepping out onto the terrace. 'I was just trying the doors.'

'Wouldn't it have been easier to come out through the side door?' I inquired.

'I dare say,' she replied vaguely, gazing intently at the bolt. 'Ye-es. Difficult to tell when they were last opened.'

'Not since the summer, I imagine,' said Sylvia.

'But I found them unlocked and unbolted just now. That's rather odd.'

'Why is it odd? Perhaps Neville unlocked them yesterday and Rogers couldn't get in to lock them again.'

'Perhaps. Although it is a little late in the year for that.' She bent down and peered at the ground. 'There are several specks of dried paint here but perhaps I did that myself just now. Rather silly of me not to look around outside first.'

'Why are you so interested in the French windows?' Sylvia asked.

'Oh, no particular reason,' said Mrs. Marchmont. She stepped back inside and banged the doors shut. Sylvia and I looked at each other and with one accord pulled them open again and went after her into the study. We found her looking about her thoughtfully.

'What is it?' I asked.

Angela frowned.

'I'm not sure,' she replied slowly. 'But something doesn't quite add up.'

'What do you mean?'

She hesitated.

'I can't quite put it into words. But I am wondering whether the doctor and Mr. Pomfrey mayn't have been mistaken about what happened.'

'Are you saying it wasn't an accident?'

'No—no, there's no reason to suppose anything of the kind. But the story of Neville's falling backwards and hitting his head doesn't ring quite true to me—I'm not sure why.'

She moved over to the fireplace and examined it closely. I sniffed the air.

'There's a strong smell of whisky,' I remarked.

'Yes, there is,' replied Angela. 'That's odd too. One would have expected the smell to have dissipated quickly, had he merely spilt a glass of it. But it smells as though someone had poured an entire bottle of the stuff all over the carpet.'

I looked towards the sideboard standing against the wall. There was a decanter standing on it, which was less than a quarter full.

'That decanter was almost full two nights ago,' I said. 'I know, because Sir Neville himself poured me a glass of it then.'

'Perhaps he drank it,' suggested Sylvia.

'That's rather a lot of whisky to drink in two days,' I said doubtfully. 'Was Sir Neville—er—inclined that way?'

'I've never seen him drink much myself but of course one never knows,' said Sylvia. 'Rogers would know, though. Perhaps we should ask him.'

Angela Marchmont was again examining the fireplace. She turned round and appeared to come to a decision.

'Look,' she said, 'I'll show you what I mean. Perhaps you can help.' To our astonishment, she lay down on the floor face upwards, with her head towards the fire and her feet pointing away from it.

'Whatever are you doing?' said Sylvia.

'This is how Neville was lying when he was found,' said Angela. 'At least, this is how I saw him when I showed Dr. Carter to the study.'

'Well?' I said. 'That seems clear enough. He tripped, fell backwards and hit his head.'

But Sylvia opened her eyes wide.

'Oh, yes, of course. I think I see what you mean,' she said slowly. 'It's all too pat.'

Angela got to her feet as gracefully as possible and brushed herself off.

'I don't understand,' I said.

'Look,' said Sylvia. She went over and stood with her back to the fireplace. 'If you fell backwards and hit your head, what would happen? Surely you would be knocked *this* way and be found in a crumpled position with your feet or, more likely your head in this case, near the fire.' She demonstrated carefully.

'Yes,' said Angela. 'The only way in which you could fall perfectly flat on your back like that would be if you fell backwards as stiffly as a board and your feet slid out from under you—but this carpet isn't slippery at all.'

'I see what you mean now but are you sure?' I said.

'No, not at all,' said Angela. 'That's why I asked you. I'm all for a rigorous approach to inquiry but I'm afraid I draw the line at cracking my own head on the mantelpiece just to test a theory.'

'Perhaps he didn't hit his head on the mantelpiece at all but on the hearth,' said Sylvia.

'I don't think so. The position of the sideboard would make that difficult.'

'Maybe somebody moved him,' I suggested.

'That's always possible,' Angela conceded. 'But according to Mr. Pomfrey, when the butler discovered the body, he immediately informed Mr. Pomfrey himself, who had the study door locked soon afterwards. I suppose the butler might have moved him but why should he?'

'Well, that's another question to ask him,' I said.

'Perhaps Neville didn't die immediately as Mr. Pomfrey said. Perhaps he moved himself into that position,' said Sylvia. This was not a nice thought but I was forced to acknowledge that it was a possibility. Angela looked doubtful, however.

'There's another thing,' she said. 'Look at this.' She indicated a vase that stood close to the edge of the mantelpiece. 'This is still standing and yet these,' she waved her hand at the poker and shovel, which were lying scattered, 'have been knocked over. Surely, if he really fell against the mantelpiece in the way we thought, this vase would have toppled to the floor too.'

I lifted the vase, which had left an imprint in the dust on the mantelpiece and remembered Rosamund's complaint about the lack of good servants.

'You're right. This hasn't moved at all,' I said.

Sylvia surveyed the room thoughtfully.

'What do you think happened, Angela?' she asked.

'That's just it. I don't know,' replied Mrs. Marchmont. 'And to tell the truth, I'm not sure that I ought to have come in here at all, or mentioned anything to you. Perhaps, after all, it would be better if we just went away and pretended we hadn't seen any of this.'

I found the implication disturbing but Sylvia nodded.

'Yes, perhaps it would,' she said.

'But if we suspect any funny business, surely it is our duty to report our suspicions,' I said.

Sylvia gave me a wry smile.

'Dear Charles! As direct and honest as ever,' she said.

Rosamund had said something very similar to me earlier and I frowned. I could not help feeling that I was being laughed at in some way.

'I don't see why we need mention this,' said Angela. I must have looked uncomfortable, because she added quickly: 'We haven't actually proved anything, you know—all we have done is to make one or two observations and speculate fruitlessly about what may or may not have happened.'

This was true but still I was not satisfied.

'All the same, I should be happier if we spoke to the solicitor or somebody about it,' I said, 'especially since you seem to be suggesting that something untoward may have occurred.'

'Why don't we speak to Rogers first?' suggested Sylvia suddenly. 'We can ask him if the—if Neville had been moved.
After all, this may all turn out to be a mare's nest and there's
no sense in raising unnecessary suspicions if we then find out
that there is a quite innocent explanation for everything.'

'I do hope you're right,' said Mrs. Marchmont. 'I should far
rather be proved an idiot than—the other.'

Fine sentiments indeed but all our arguing proved irrelevant because the next moment Mr. Pomfrey and Dr. Carter
entered the room.

CHAPTER EIGHT

A H,' SAID MR. Pomfrey, clearly taken aback to find the study already occupied. 'We—er—have come to—er—'

'I beg your pardon,' said the doctor briskly, ignoring the solicitor's palpable embarrassment, 'but I should like to examine this fireplace more closely.' He strode forward.

'Hm—ah—yes,' said Mr. Pomfrey, in an agony of discretion. Evidently, finding three guests in the study had not formed part of his plans.

Dr. Carter peered at the edge of the mantelpiece and appeared to spot something. He dabbed at it with his forefinger and sniffed it delicately. 'Yes—hair oil, I should say. That seems straightforward enough.'

I was momentarily surprised at the revelation that Sir Neville had used hair oil. I had not thought him the type.

'Did you say that the body had not been moved?' the doctor asked, turning to the solicitor.

'That was certainly the impression I received from the butler,' replied Mr. Pomfrey.

'I see. Perhaps we should have him in here, to clear up the matter.'

Before anybody could reply, the doctor rang the bell.

'Is something the matter?' I asked. Mr. Pomfrey bridled a little.

'Ah—Dr. Carter merely wished to take a closer look at the scene of the accident, as he has some questions he would like answered. I do not believe there is any real cause for concern, however,' he said.

Rogers appeared, looking somewhat apprehensive.

'May I be of assistance, sir?' he asked.

'I think you may, Rogers,' said Dr. Carter. 'I should like to hear your account of how Sir Neville was found this morning.'

Rogers swallowed and trembled.

'Pardon me, sir but this has all been very upsetting,' he said unhappily.

'Yes, yes, of course,' said Mr. Pomfrey encouragingly. 'Indeed we are all very shocked by the occurrence and are trying our best to discover the exact circumstances of Sir Neville's unfortunate accident. That is why we require your help. We should like to know exactly what happened this morning.'

'Well, sir,' said the old man, 'The first I knew of the matter was early this morning, when one of the housemaids came to me and said she had found the study door locked and so was unable to enter the room to sweep it. I went along with her to see for myself and it was just as she had said. There was no reply when I knocked, so at first I thought the study must be unoccupied. On further inquiry, however, I found from the servants that Sir Neville had not been seen that morning, nor had his bed been slept in and I became somewhat concerned.'

'Did it strike you as strange that the door should be locked?'

'Yes sir, it was very strange and made me very uneasy. I was anxious to get into the study as soon as possible. Eventually I remembered that there were several odd keys locked away in a drawer in my room, so I had them fetched and fortunately one of them fitted. When we entered the study we found Sir Neville lying dead by the fireplace.' He took a handkerchief out of his pocket and mopped his brow. 'Pardon me sir but I am not accustomed to this sort of thing,' he said.

'Quite, quite,' said Mr. Pomfrey sympathetically.

'If you used a spare key to enter the study, then the usual key must have been missing from the inside of the door,' I said. 'Otherwise the spare key would not have worked.'

'Oh no, sir,' replied the butler. 'I ought to have mentioned that the key was in the lock and we had to fetch a length of strong wire to push it onto the floor from the other side before we could try any of the spare keys.'

Mr. Pomfrey nodded.

'Yes, I have both keys here in my pocket,' he said. Turning back to Rogers, he said: 'When you found Sir Neville, did you approach or touch him at all?'

'I had to approach him, sir, as he was not visible from the doorway. He was hidden by the desk and the easy-chair that is placed to one side of the fire. I approached quite near to him, as I thought it possible that he had merely hurt himself but one look was enough to tell me that there was nothing to be done.'

'And what did you do then?'

'Why, sir, I locked the door and came straightaway and reported the matter to you. I did not think it my place to break the news myself to Lady Strickland.'

'Did you move the body at all?'

'No, sir. I never even touched him.'

'When you returned with me to the study, he was in the same position in which you had left him?'

'Yes, sir.'

'I see. Very good, Rogers, you may go.'

'Just one moment,' said Mrs. Marchmont gently. 'I have one or two questions, if I may.'

The butler paused obediently.

'You are responsible for locking up the house at night, are you not?'

'I am, madam,' replied the butler.

'At what time?'

'The usual time is ten o'clock but I do my rounds later, at eleven o'clock, when we have guests. Some people like to take an evening stroll on the terrace, you see.'

'Do you check all the doors every night? Even those that perhaps have not been opened for some time?'

'Every one, madam. Sir Neville is—was most particular about it. We often have guests here and you never know when one of them might take it into his head to unlock a door without telling anybody—begging your pardon, madam.'

'Did you check them all last night?'

'Yes, madam. I made sure they were all locked as usual—all except the French windows in here. Sir Neville came here after dinner and locked himself in. He said he had no further need for me that evening and did not want to be disturbed.'

'Was it normal for him to lock himself in?' asked Mr. Pomfrey.

'Not *normal*, exactly,' said Rogers, considering. 'But he had done it one or twice before, usually when he had something important to do and didn't want anybody to disturb him. I recall he said once that he had done it out of absent-mindedness—he was thinking so hard about the business at hand that he did not realize he had done it.'

'So you don't know whether or not the French windows were locked last night?' said Angela.

'No, madam, but as Sir Neville had been adamant that he was to be left in peace and as he had locked the study door, I did not feel I could insist on completing my rounds. I mentioned it to Lady Strickland and she agreed that I should not disturb him. The French windows had been locked the night before and I could see no reason why Sir Neville should open them, so I let the matter lie. I hope no harm has come of it,' he concluded anxiously.

'Not as far as I know,' replied Mrs. Marchmont. 'I have just one more question.' She indicated the whisky decanter on the sideboard. 'When did you last re-fill this?'

'It would have been on Wednesday, madam,' replied Rogers.

'Today is Saturday and there is hardly any left. Does that strike you as normal? Pardon me for asking but did Sir Neville generally drink whisky in this sort of quantity?'

Rogers looked shocked.

'No indeed!' he replied. 'I have always found him to be a very temperate gentleman. He would take a small glass before dinner and occasionally another after, usually with soda. I don't know why the whisky should have gone down so quickly. Perhaps he had company.'

'I had a glass of it on Thursday,' I said, 'and the decanter was almost full then. Did anybody visit Sir Neville in his study after that?'

'I did,' said Mr. Pomfrey. 'I spent some time in here with Sir Neville yesterday afternoon but I had no whisky. I'm afraid I did not notice whether the decanter was full or not. I don't suppose you noticed it, Rogers?'

'I do not remember it in particular but I am sure I should have noticed if it was nearly empty,' replied the butler.

'Thank you Rogers,' said Mrs. Marchmont. 'You may go.'

'May I ask what this is all about?' asked the doctor, when the butler had left the room. He had been listening with interest. 'All these questions about locked doors and whisky decanters—what are you getting at?'

'Dear me,' said Mrs. Marchmont wryly. 'I appear to have been defeated by circumstances this afternoon. I had hoped to do a little quiet thinking on this whole matter rather than create a fuss that might prove both dangerous and unnecessary, but what with one thing and another I couldn't have drawn more attention to myself had I stood on the lawn and waved a red flag.' She sighed. 'Very well, I suppose I must explain. But first, doctor, would you have any objection to telling us why you were so interested in the fireplace?'

'I suppose there's no harm in it,' replied Dr. Carter, with a glance at Mr. Pomfrey, 'since I have the feeling that we may be thinking on the same lines. I merely felt that the position in which Sir Neville was found did not appear to tally with the accounts of the accident that apparently befell him and I wished to take a closer look at this room. Between ourselves, it would have been almost impossible for Sir Neville to have hit his head on the mantelpiece and fallen so. Ah,' he said, looking round at the three of us. 'I see by your faces that this is not a surprise to you.'

'Not entirely,' admitted Angela. 'I must confess that I had some doubts this morning when I accompanied you to the study and saw Neville lying there. It all seemed too neat, somehow, although of course I'm not an expert in these matters. So I came back here this afternoon and was just doing a little snooping about on my own account when I was caught in the act by Sylvia and Mr. Knox, who probably thought me quite mad.'

'I gather from your earlier question to Rogers that you found the French windows unlocked,' said Mr. Pomfrey.

'Yes,' said Angela. 'The key was in the lock as you see it and the bolts were unfastened.'

'Do you mean that somebody could have come in from outside?' asked Sylvia.

'Well, it did occur to me, certainly,' replied Angela. 'When I tried them they were a little stiff but not overly so. It was difficult to tell whether or not they had been opened recently.'

The doctor went over to the French windows to look for himself.

'Yes,' he said. 'The key's there all right. And you say the bolts were drawn? That means they were unlocked from inside. We shall have to find out who did it.'

'Sir Neville would be the most natural person, surely,' I said.

'Probably. And what about the whisky?'

Mrs. Marchmont explained about the strong smell of whisky. Mr. Pomfrey inhaled deeply through his nose.

'Now you come to mention it, there is something,' he said.

'This is all very well,' I said, 'but if I understand correctly, what you are implying is that somebody arranged Sir Neville's body next to the mantelpiece, knocked the fire-irons over, sprinkled whisky all over the carpet to give the impression he had drunk too much—'

'—smeared hair oil on the mantelpiece,' put in the doctor helpfully.

'—then left through the French windows,' I finished. 'But for what exactly?'

'It's a shocking waste of good whisky, certainly,' murmured the doctor. He recollected himself and had the grace to look ashamed.

There was a pause.

'Very well,' I said. 'Since no-one seems to want to say the word, I shall. What we are really saying is that this was not an accident at all but murder.'

CHAPTER NINE

I AM NOT quite sure what reaction I expected when I said it but I was slightly disconcerted when everyone, including Sylvia, merely nodded sagely.

'A murder that has been hurriedly and clumsily disguised to *look* like an accident,' I continued.

'It certainly looks as though that might be a possibility,' said Dr. Carter. 'Although of course there is no proof—just a few pieces of circumstantial evidence.' He counted off on his fingers: 'One, the position of the body. Two, the whisky decanter. Three, the French windows. Is there anything else?'

Angela explained about the vase on the mantelpiece.

'Hm, that is something else to consider, certainly,' said the doctor.

'Then how did he die, if not by hitting his head?' I asked.

'Oh, he certainly received an injury to the back of the head that killed him instantaneously,' the doctor assured us. 'But that could equally have been the result of a deliberate blow.'

Mr. Pomfrey coughed.

'Let us return to the French windows,' he said. 'Mrs. Marchmont, I believe you said they were rather stiff when you opened them.'

'Yes,' said Angela, 'but not *very* difficult to open, so I'm not sure we can deduce anything from that. There were some specks of loose paint on the ground outside but I may have done that myself when I opened the doors. I am afraid I have ruined any evidence that might have been got that way.'

'If the doors were open then anyone could have got in from outside,' said Sylvia.

'It seems so,' replied Mr. Pomfrey.

'But who unlocked them from the inside?' I said. 'Surely the most obvious person is Sir Neville himself. He must have been expecting someone.'

'Not necessarily,' said Angela. 'Anybody could have come in during the day yesterday and opened them. It's unlikely that it would have been noticed until Rogers did his rounds.'

'Just a moment,' said Dr. Carter. 'We are running ahead of ourselves. The fact that the French windows were unlocked is unimportant unless there is clear evidence that Sir Neville was killed deliberately. They are not, in themselves, evidence of foul play. If it was an accident, then we must accept that there is a perfectly innocent explanation for it. At present, therefore, the French windows are merely a distraction.'

'That is very true,' said Mr. Pomfrey. 'The question is, do we have enough evidence to indicate that foul play has occurred?'

'No,' admitted the doctor, 'but the evidence we *have* found is very suggestive. There is one thing I should like to clear up before we proceed further, however. The butler states that the body was not moved but we have not yet spoken to the house-maid. I should like to be certain that their accounts agree. The butler is an old fellow and perhaps he moved Sir Neville and merely forgot about it, or didn't wish to get into trouble over it.'

This seemed reasonable.

'Perhaps I should speak to her alone?' suggested Dr. Carter. 'Since it seems she was very upset this morning, if she is questioned by five people at once it may prove too much for her.'

This was agreed to and the doctor went off, leaving the four of us to gaze round the room and at one another. I stared at one of the African artefacts that Sir Neville had proudly shown me only two days ago, a statue of an elongated kneeling woman, and remembered our mysterious conversation. Sylvia was the first to speak, voicing my own unspoken question.

'What if the housemaid confirms Rogers's story? What then?'

Mr. Pomfrey coughed.

'Er—I must confess that I am not entirely sure. I expect her to support the butler's story, of course. Indeed, I should be astonished if she does not, given Rogers's position of authority among the servants. However, if she does confirm it—ahem—yes, the fact that Dr. Carter is here makes things rather more difficult,' he finished obliquely.

'You mean that he will insist on sending for the police, I suppose,' said Sylvia.

'But of course we want the criminal to be caught,' I said, 'if there is indeed a criminal at large. Other houses in the neighbourhood may be in danger.'

Nobody replied. A few minutes later, Dr. Carter returned.

'It's no go I'm afraid,' he said briefly. 'The housemaid—Ellen is her name, by the way—is quite certain that neither she nor Rogers touched the body. She says when they finally entered the study, the lamp was still on and Sir Neville was lying by the fireplace exactly as we saw him. The butler then ushered her out of the room and locked the door, as we have already heard. She says she saw him speaking to Mr. Pomfrey almost immediately afterwards.'

'What now?' asked Angela.

'I don't pretend to know what happened but I'm afraid I must insist on this room being locked for the moment,' replied the doctor. 'Pomfrey, you and I must decide what to do. I think we have no choice but to call in the police, or at least the coroner. I wonder—you know Colonel Tremayne, the chief constable, don't you? A friend of Sir Neville's too, I believe. Let us start with him. He will send someone discreet. We don't want a crowd of yokels gawping outside.'

'Yes, Tremayne is a good man,' murmured Mr. Pomfrey. 'Let us hope that he decides this is all a mare's nest.'

Carter saw us out of the room, locked it and disappeared down the passage, deep in conversation with the solicitor. It was clear that we had been dismissed and that the forces of officialdom were about to take over.

'I must go and see Rosamund,' said Angela and left us.

'Come into the conservatory,' said Sylvia. We found the room unoccupied and sat down to reflect on the astonishing revelations of the past hour or two. Sylvia bit her lip in thought.

'I wonder if it was Neville who opened the French windows, or someone else,' she said.

'I expect it was Sir Neville himself,' I said. 'I must say that on reflection I am not entirely convinced by this foul play theory. It seems to rest on so little. If somebody did come from outside to see Sir Neville, then who was it? And why visit at so late an hour? Was it a secret visit? In that case, what was the reason? And how on earth did it end in murder?'

'Perhaps it was someone who bore a grudge against him,' said Sylvia. 'Neville was a magistrate you know.'

'But then why should he open the French windows and let them in?'

'I don't know. Perhaps the visitor knocked and asked to be admitted and Neville had no reason to suspect that any harm would come to him.'

An idea struck me.

'What if it wasn't Sir Neville who opened the French windows at all but a servant with evil intentions? Let us say he had an accomplice or accomplices outside the house and the intention was burglary. Now, what happens? The servant informs his associates that the French windows on the ground floor will be unlocked and that the way will be clear, let's say after midnight. But the plans go awry—the household not only stays up later than expected but one member of it has also locked himself firmly in the study. The gang arrive, are confronted by the owner of the house and silence him. They arrange the body to make it look like an accident and flee empty-handed.'

'I can think of several objections to that,' replied Sylvia. 'If they wanted to get away quickly and quietly, why should they bother making it look like an accident? And if the motive was burglary, then why didn't they take anything? One would think that if they were desperate enough to resort to murder, then they would at least have stolen something to make it worth their while. There are one or two rather valuable paintings on the walls in the study, yet they were left untouched. And,' she finished, 'we didn't stay up late at all, if you remember. The row between Gwen and Joan rather spoilt things and we all went to bed.'

I had been warming to my theory but I was forced to concede that Sylvia had a point.

'Well, we shall have to wait and see what the police say,' I said. 'Who knows, perhaps they will find conclusive proof that it was an accident. God knows, it will be hard enough on Rosamund having to deal with her husband's death but even more so if it turns out that it was murder.'

'Oh yes, poor Rosamund,' said Sylvia suddenly. 'How awful of us. Here we are having a high old time debating who may or may not have killed Neville as though it were some sort of detective game, while she is having to face the fact that she has lost her husband and is now a widow.'

I started. Sylvia was right. That was exactly what we had been doing. It was not a game though but a ghastly reality. We looked at each other guiltily.

'I feel rather a worm,' she said.

'So do I,' I said.

'Let's go in to tea.'

I laughed.

'Tea!' I said. 'Our comfort and our joy. If England should ever fall and the race be all but wiped out, it is certain that the last few surviving Englishmen will be found at some faraway outpost, drinking tea as though nothing had happened!'

It was not until we were all seated at dinner that the chief constable arrived, accompanied by an inspector. Rosamund had remained in her room and her place had been taken by Angela Marchmont, who attempted to keep us all as cheerful as possible. Nonetheless, we were all horridly conscious of the empty place at the other end of the table, in which Sir Neville had sat only the evening before.

We were all toying listlessly with our soup when Rogers came in and informed Mrs. Marchmont in a low tone that the chief constable had just arrived and was in conference with Lady Strickland. The surprise of some of the party at the arrival of the police was nothing to the surprise of three of us in particular on finding out that, instead of bringing with him a local inspector, the chief constable had in fact wired to Scotland Yard to send one of their best men, one Inspector Jameson.

'The police?' cried Gwen MacMurray. 'Why on earth are the police here?'

Angela, Sylvia and I looked at each other in astonishment, all clearly thinking the same thing: Scotland Yard! It must indeed be a serious case! Angela was so distracted for a moment that she accidentally laid her napkin down in the soup and there was a brief interlude as Rogers fussed over her. However, she was soon called upon to reply to the urgent questioning of those who had not been present in the study earlier.

'Come on, Angela,' said Bobs. 'No secrets now. What's all this about?'

Mrs. Marchmont recounted the events of that afternoon, to the general astonishment and consternation of the table.

'What! You're saying that a gang of vile murderers got into the house and bashed poor old Neville on the head!' exclaimed Hugh MacMurray. 'I don't believe it. How could they have got in without being seen or heard by someone?'

His wife gave a little shriek.

'We could all have been murdered in our beds!' she cried. 'Hugh, we must leave at once. This house isn't safe.'

Joan gave her a withering look.

'They can't get away with it, surely,' she said. 'The police must catch them soon. After all, this house is practically in the middle of nowhere. They must have been spotted by somebody. Any strangers would stick out a mile.'

'They might not have been strangers,' said Sylvia. 'It might have been an attack by somebody whom Neville encountered as a magistrate, out for revenge.'

'I can't think who could have borne such a grudge,' said Joan. 'Tivenham is hardly the East End of London, you know. It's the most peaceful place you can imagine. Why, the most

serious crimes to happen around here are poaching and public drunkenness. We had a case a few years ago where a local
farmer shot his wife but there was no mystery to that and it
was all cleared up very quickly.'

'Well,' I said, 'if there is anything untoward about Sir Neville's death—which I am not convinced of myself—the police
will solve the mystery.'

'Will they want to ask us any questions?' asked Gwen. 'That's
what happens in detective stories. Oh! I'm sure I shall be much
too frightened to think properly and when they ask me where
I was at the time of the murder I shan't know what to say, or
give the wrong answer, or something and that will make them
suspicious, even though I know nothing about it.' Her voice
rose to a shrill pitch. 'What if they arrest me? Boopsie, you
must stay with me when they are questioning me. You mustn't
let them try to trick me or trap me.'

'Do shut up, Gwen, there's a good girl,' said Bobs.

Just then, a message arrived to say that Colonel Tremayne,
the chief constable, would be grateful if the party could spare
him a few minutes in the drawing-room after dinner. Gwen
MacMurray gasped and opened her mouth to speak but
caught Bobs's eye and thought better of it.

Dinner was finished very quickly after that. Whether or
not we wished to admit it, I think we were all eager to hear
what the chief constable had to say. Of one accord, ladies and
gentlemen alike rose and hurried into the drawing-room. We
found it already occupied by two people: a large military type
who looked like nothing so much as a chief constable and

Rosamund, who waved away our expressions of concern and sympathy. She was pale and had dark circles around her eyes but otherwise seemed to be dealing with the shock bravely.

'Please, I'm quite all right, really,' she said. 'Don't worry about me. The most important thing now is to find out what happened to poor Neville. I can hardly believe that it wasn't an accident but it must be true because Colonel Tremayne and Inspector Jameson tell me so.'

'Now now, Lady Strickland,' said Colonel Tremayne, 'we have not yet reached any conclusion. Jameson and a couple of my men are examining the study closely and I expect we shall hear from them shortly.'

'Why have you called in Scotland Yard?' asked Joan.

'A mere matter of routine, my dear,' replied Colonel Tremayne airily. I saw Angela Marchmont wrinkle her brow in puzzlement.

'I think all of us would like to know what exactly is going on,' said Bobs, to several nods of agreement.

'Certainly,' said the chief constable. 'That is why I wished to speak to you all. At present, we have reason to believe that Sir Neville's death was not an accident. Sir Neville has now been removed from the house and Dr. Carter will perform a closer examination, which should give us a better idea of what happened to him. It is a pity that so many people have visited the scene of the—er—occurrence and perhaps destroyed valuable evidence but since no suspicion arose at first I suppose it can't be helped.'

I glanced guiltily at Sylvia and Angela.

'One thing I should like to request,' continued Colonel Tremayne, 'is that you all remain here in this house, at least for the next day or two.'

'But why?' asked Gwen. 'None of us saw or heard the thieves.'

'And surely the fewer people there are in the house the easier it will be for your men to conduct their investigation.' added Joan.

The chief constable smiled blandly.

'Oh, don't worry about them: you will hardly notice they are here,' he said. 'But all the same, I should be grateful if you would all remain here. Once the examination of the scene of this unfortunate occurrence is complete, Inspector Jameson will no doubt wish to speak to you all, in order to get an idea of the sequence of events last night. You say you all saw nothing. However, it is possible that one or more of you may hold a clue to which you yourself attach no importance but which may prove highly significant. We cannot tell until we have spoken to you all tomorrow and ascertained the full facts of the matter.'

He then rose and excused himself, saying that he wished to speak to the inspector.

'After that, I shall leave the case in his capable hands,' he said. 'Scotland Yard think very highly of him and—what is almost as important—we can rely utterly on his discretion.'

It was the second time I had heard someone mention discretion in connection with Sir Neville's death. But where was the need for it? If a crime had been committed, then it was essential that the criminal be brought to book as soon as possible. I was perplexed.

The rest of the evening passed in a desultory fashion. Nobody wanted to play at cards and it was hardly seemly to put on the gramophone. Rosamund sat by the window, staring out into the darkness, while Bobs, annoyed at having been left out of the events of the afternoon, went out to see if he could find out what was happening. He soon returned.

'No luck,' he said. 'Our worthy constabulary have positioned a large, impassive slab of granite in the shape of a policeman at the entrance to the study passage. "Good evening, sir", it said. "I'm afraid I'm under orders not to let anybody past at the moment." So I was forced to give up and come back here.'

'Yes,' I said. 'I tried the same thing myself earlier but got no further than the hall before I was politely sent on my way.'

'I wonder if they will find anything,' said Sylvia. 'After all—'

She broke off as the drawing-room door opened and a spare man with an alert expression entered. He introduced himself as Inspector Jameson.

'I must apologize to Lady Strickland and the rest of you for keeping you out of part of the house,' he said. 'However, I'm afraid procedures must be followed and I would like to ask you to be patient while we complete our investigation.'

'Of course you must do your duty,' said Rosamund. There was a general murmur of agreement.

'Have you found anything?' asked Joan bluntly.

'I won't be able to tell you that for definite until we've finished and we won't do that until tomorrow. It's too dark to examine the grounds in detail now, so that will have to wait until the morning. I am also going to try your patience a little further by asking to speak to each of you, to try and build up a picture of the events of last night. I shall leave you now but I'll be back early tomorrow. In the meantime, I have left a constable stationed here—we can't be too careful, after what has happened.'

He smiled round pleasantly at the assembled company and departed. Bobs looked after him approvingly.

'Seems like a sound enough chap,' he remarked. 'One of our sort. Wonder if he's any relation to old "Topper" Jameson. You remember him, don't you, Charles? He was in the form above us at Eton. I think he went into the Foreign Office.'

I remembered the boy in question but had no idea whether he had any relatives who had gone into the police force.

Sylvia went across to where Rosamund was sitting.

'You look very tired, darling,' she said. 'It's been a simply ghastly day, hasn't it?'

'Yes,' said Rosamund. 'Yes, I am tired, now you mention it. I hadn't realized it before. And I'm cold and stiff and aching all over. Perhaps I shall go to bed.'

'I hope you're not going to be ill,' said Joan, with concern.

'No, no, I'm not ill but I should like to sleep. Don't worry about me, darlings,' she said, addressing the sympathetic faces that were turned towards her. 'The doctor has given me something to make me sleep. A night's rest and I shall be ready to face whatever lies ahead tomorrow.'

She lifted her chin up in determined fashion and left the room. I felt rather tired myself after the happenings of the day and soon afterwards headed off to bed myself.

That night, however, sleep eluded me. The events of the day whirled round and round in my head and kept me wide awake. It seemed incredible that so many extraordinary things could have happened in less than twenty-four hours. That my host had been found dead in his study was bad enough but that he was suspected of having been murdered and the police called in was still worse! Thoughts rushed headlong through my mind in chaotic fashion and made sleep impossible.

At last, in desperation, I got up, with some intention of fetching a book from the library to while away the small hours. Leaving my room, I made my way down the stairs with the help of the dim light that was left burning all night in the hall. At the bottom of the stairs I hesitated for a moment.

'Good evening, sir, may I help you?' came a voice to my right. I jumped guiltily and turned to look into the placid face of the police constable who had prevented me from entering the study passage earlier in the evening.

'Ah, good evening,' I said. 'I was just going to look for a book in the library. I couldn't sleep, you see. It's been rather an odd day,' I concluded somewhat feebly.

'Very understandable,' said the constable. 'I always find that a cup of hot milk does the trick, myself.'

'Ah—is that so?' I replied. 'But I think I shall try the book first.'

'Each to his own, sir,' said the policeman comfortably.

Feeling rather foolish, I went into the library, picked up a book without much regard to its contents and hurried back upstairs, bidding the man goodnight as I passed. After trying to concentrate on the book for a few minutes, however, I soon found my eyes feeling heavy—whether because of the book itself or my foray downstairs, and after persevering unsuccessfully for a few more minutes I thankfully turned off the lamp and fell asleep.

CHAPTER TEN

T HE NEXT DAY I rose early and went outside for a stroll, eager, I must confess, to see what the police were up to. Jameson and his men had already arrived and were busying themselves about the terrace and the flower beds and lawns close to the house. I struck out towards the ha-ha, from where I could see what was happening without getting in the way and without seeming too curious. I soon found that someone else had had the same idea.

'Ha! Good morning,' said Hugh MacMurray. 'I see you're keeping an eye on these police chappies, like me. It's just like a detective novel, what?'

'Nothing could have been further from my thoughts,' I replied stiffly. 'I was merely taking a walk to clear my head before breakfast.'

'Yes, yes, that's a good story,' he said jovially. 'I say, what do you think they will find?'

He seemed unduly cheerful for a man whose closest relative had just died but then I remembered that he was due to inherit a substantial sum of money and gave him a look of disdain. He appeared not to notice it but prattled on about the lurid penny dreadfuls that evidently made the bulk of his reading. I was relieved when we were joined by Joan, who was giving the dogs their morning walk.

'I wish the police would finish their work and tell us what is happening,' she said. 'I feel somehow as though we are all being closely observed, like—like specimens in a glass jar or something.'

'Yes, I feel a little the same myself,' I agreed.

'One thing I do know,' she said. 'The police have been asking the servants about the whisky decanter. It must be an important clue.'

'How can they prove anything from that?' asked MacMurray.

'I don't know. Perhaps they have found some finger-prints on it, which will lead them to the criminal.'

'Oh yes,' said MacMurray eagerly. 'They can do wonderful things with brushes and powders these days, so I understand. The decanter might look perfectly clean to you or me but just watch when the police get their kit out—a dollop of the old powder and bingo! A whole set of clear finger-prints that were invisible before. The murderer doesn't stand a chance.'

'I hope you are right,' I said.

A police constable moved slowly towards us, scanning the ground closely as he went.

'I say!' said MacMurray, as he approached. The man looked up.

'Good morning, sir,' he said.

'Anything at all we can do in the investigating line? I mean to say, we could look for footprints or something if it would help. I've always wanted to do a spot of detecting and—well, anything to help old Neville, of course.'

The policeman smiled indulgently.

'That won't be necessary, sir,' he replied. 'The police have everything in hand. I dare say the inspector will ask to speak to you later.'

He nodded and moved off.

'That's a shame!' said MacMurray. 'Still, I think I shall stroll over to the terrace and try to find out what they are doing.' He was as good as his word. I was not especially keen to be associated with the fellow, so I headed back into the house in search of breakfast and dampened my curiosity as best I could by immersing myself in a book until lunch-time.

Shortly after that meal, we were told that Inspector Jameson had requested our presence in the drawing-room at half-past two, as he had something to say to us. Mr. Pomfrey had returned that morning, in his capacity as family solicitor and we found him seated in a comfortable chair, looking rather like a benevolent brownie.

'First of all, I should like to thank you for your forbearance so far,' began the inspector. 'This has been a terrible and tragic event and it can't have been made any easier by having the police nosing around. But I shan't keep you in suspense any longer. I'm afraid that our preliminary inquiries show that Sir Neville was indeed murdered.'

Gwen MacMurray gasped. I glanced across at Rosamund, who looked pale but unsurprised. Evidently Inspector Jameson had informed her of the fact earlier.

'How do you know?' asked Bobs.

'There are a number of clues,' said the inspector. 'I can't reveal them all but the most important one is that we have found what we believe to be the murder weapon.'

A shiver ran through the room.

'Yes,' he continued. 'It was a primitive wooden carving of a woman, which stood upon a shelf in the study. Perhaps you have seen it. It had been wiped clean but a tiny knot in the wood had one or two hairs caught in it and there were also unmistakable traces of Sir Neville's hair oil, as well as—other traces.'

I remembered staring at the very same statue the previous afternoon. It had not occurred to me for a moment that I was looking at a weapon that had been used to kill a man.

'Then he didn't hit his head on the mantelpiece at all,' said Sylvia.

'Certainly not,' said Jameson. 'We believe he was hit from behind as he sat at his desk and then arranged by the fireplace. Some marks were found on the carpet which indicate that something large and heavy was dragged across the room from the desk.'

The carpet was a patterned one, I remembered, which would explain why we had not spotted the marks ourselves.

'Why have you been asking the servants about the whisky decanter?' asked Joan. 'What's so important about it?'

'As I understand some of you discovered yesterday,' said the inspector, 'a quantity of whisky seems to have been spilt on the carpet—possibly to create a strong scent of alcohol in the study and make it appear as though Sir Neville had fallen after having drunk too much of it.'

'Might Sir Neville have spilt the stuff himself accidentally?' I asked.

The inspector turned towards me.

'We considered that possibility,' he replied. 'However, after testing the decanter for finger-prints, we were forced to abandon that theory.'

'Why?' I asked.

The inspector smiled.

'Because there were no finger-prints at all on the decanter. It had been wiped clean, as had the whisky glass.'

There was a pause as the information sank in. I looked across at Rosamund, who was white-faced and breathing rapidly. Poor Rosamund, I thought, having to listen to these sordid details. I caught her eye and she smiled wanly at me.

Angela Marchmont spoke.

'What about the French windows?' she asked. 'I'm afraid I put my grimy hands all over them yesterday but were there any other finger-prints?'

'The evidence on the outside handle is inconclusive,' said Jameson, 'but on the inside one there appears to be only one set—presumably yours, Mrs. Marchmont. I should like to take an impression of your finger-prints, to compare with those on the inside handle, if you would permit me.'

I had opened the doors myself from the terrace the day before. But who had closed them again? It must have been Angela, I supposed.

'Yes of course,' said Angela. 'We shall do that whenever you like. And I suppose it would be helpful to you to take everybody else's, too. But about the French windows: if only my finger-prints are on the inside, then doesn't that mean that someone wiped the handle clean before leaving, just as they did with the decanter?'

'It would seem so,' replied the inspector.

'I must say, it's a damned odd, clumsy way of going about things,' said Bobs, frowning. 'If the murderer meant to make it seem like an accident, he didn't do it very well.'

Jameson nodded.

'Yes. It very much looks as though he were in a hurry. And that brings us to the time of the deed. I have asked you all to gather here because I believe you can help me narrow down the time at which the crime was committed.' He looked at his notebook. 'Dr. Carter says that when he examined Sir Neville, he had been dead for at least eight hours and probably longer. That puts the time of death at no later than half-past one or so. However, we don't yet know when Sir Neville was last seen alive.'

'I saw him last shortly after dinner,' said Bobs. 'He came to the drawing-room but left soon afterwards. In fact, as far as I know, he went to his study then and never came out again.'

Several people nodded in agreement.

'At what time was this?' asked the inspector.

'I haven't the faintest idea, I'm afraid,' replied Bobs cheerfully.

'It was shortly after nine o'clock,' said Simon Gale. I was startled to find him sitting close to me, as I had not even realized he was in the room.

'Are you certain of that?' asked Jameson. Gale nodded.

'I am in the habit of noticing such things,' he said.

Jameson looked at his notes again.

'Mr. Gale's account agrees with that of Rogers, the butler, who says he saw Sir Neville entering the study at about that time.'

'He was alive at least an hour later than that,' I said suddenly. The inspector looked up.

'Indeed?'

'Yes,' I said. 'Of course! Don't you remember, Rosamund? You wanted him to come and play Consequences. We went along to the study and knocked but he wouldn't come out.'

'Oh!' said Rosamund, sitting up straight. 'Yes, of course. I'd quite forgotten.'

'Tell me exactly what happened, please,' said Jameson.

I explained about the game of Consequences and how Sir Neville had refused to take part.

'What did he say, exactly?'

'I can't remember his exact words,' said Rosamund, 'but it was something like "No, do carry on, I must finish these papers this evening". Something like that. He didn't say anything important. At any rate, one can't hold a sensible conversation through a locked door, so we gave it up and returned to the drawing-room.'

'And what time was that?'

'Oh, I don't know,' replied Rosamund. 'I never know the time. Charles will remember. Or Hugh. You were there, too, don't you remember, Hugh? We met you coming in from the terrace.'

'I think it was at about a quarter to eleven,' I said.

'And none of you spoke to him after that? Very well, in that case, I think we can say with some certainty that Sir Neville died after a quarter to eleven and before half-past one. Now, I understand that the house was locked up at eleven o'clock, with the exception of the French windows. It therefore seems reasonable to assume that the assailant—or assailants—entered the house that way, especially since Rogers swears that the house keys remained in his coat pocket all the time. We therefore need to discover who it was who opened the French windows to enable the murderer to enter.'

'We thought it might have been Sir Neville himself,' I said. 'Perhaps he was expecting someone for reasons unknown and wanted to ensure that that someone would not be seen when he arrived.'

'But who could it have been?' said Joan. 'Inspector, the theory has been put forward that it was a revenge attack by somebody who had encountered Neville in the magistrate's court but that simply won't wash. There are no people of that sort around here. And as for burglary as a motive,' she continued, 'why, anybody can see that nothing has been taken. No, that's no good either.'

'Well, we shall see,' said the inspector non-committally. 'We must, of course, investigate all avenues. Let us go back to Sir Neville. Did he seem his usual self on the night of the murder?'

We all looked at each other, then Gwen MacMurray spoke up for the first time.

'No, he didn't,' she said. 'He was rather down. He had been depressed for a couple of days, in fact.'

'Do you have any idea of the reason?'

I remembered again Sir Neville's mysterious words to me on my first evening at Sissingham, when he had talked of liars and schemers, but held my tongue.

'I think we all assumed it was something to do with business,' said Bobs, 'but perhaps Gale or Pomfrey can tell you more about that than I can.'

'I do not believe this is the place to reveal details of Sir Neville's business affairs,' said Mr. Pomfrey. 'Nonetheless, I see no harm in stating that there was no particular cause for concern as far as I am aware.'

'No, there was not,' agreed Gale. 'It is no secret that Sir Neville was considering entering into a gold-mining venture in South Africa with Mr. Knox and Lord Haverford and that the preliminary business was taking up much of his time. However, there was no reason for him to be despondent about his affairs.'

'Of course not!' exclaimed Gwen. 'If there had been, I'm sure he would have confided in Hugh. Hugh and he were terribly close, you know.'

I saw Inspector Jameson turn his attention to Gwen as though he had not noticed her before and study her carefully.

'Have you any idea what might have been troubling Sir Neville?' he asked her gently.

Gwen tossed her head.

'I'm sure I don't know,' she said, in a tone of voice that plainly meant, 'I have a jolly good idea but I shan't tell.'

'Very well,' said the inspector. 'That is all for the present, although I may wish to speak to some or all of you alone later on.'

Gwen shivered pleasurably.

The inspector bade us all a good afternoon and left the room. Under normal circumstances, we should all have talked about the murder at length but as Rosamund was present this would, of course, have been highly insensitive. Gradually, therefore, we all drifted out of the room, leaving Rosamund in conversation with Mr. Pomfrey.

I was writing a letter in my room some time later, when I was drawn to the window by the sound of running footsteps, which seemed to come from the terrace below. I peered out but could see nothing. However, further out on the lawn I saw Bobs, Sylvia and Angela Marchmont all staring in the same direction, towards the house. I ran downstairs and joined them.

'Hallo,' I said. 'From the window you looked as though you had all stared at a Gorgon and been turned to stone. What is it?'

'The most extraordinary thing,' said Bobs. 'I—'

He stopped, as the police constable I had seen that morning suddenly erupted from the French windows leading into the study, bolted round the corner and entered the house through the side door.

'What on earth is he doing?' I asked in astonishment.

'You find us as perplexed as you are, old thing. We were just taking a gentle stroll around the grounds to clear away the cobwebs, when all of a sudden that fellow came haring out of the house and in through the French windows. A few minutes later, he came out again, as you saw.'

'It seems an awfully odd way of investigating a murder,' said Sylvia.

'Oh, of course!' murmured Angela Marchmont, half under her breath.

We turned to her inquiringly.

'Yes,' she went on. 'It all makes sense now. I didn't understand the potatoes at all.'

She saw our surprised faces and laughed.

'No, I haven't gone mad—not quite yet, anyhow. It's just that earlier on, I saw one of the policemen hauling what looked like a large sack of potatoes towards the study and wondered why. But of course it's obvious now.'

'Not to me,' said Sylvia.

'Don't you see? The sack of potatoes represents Neville. They are trying to re-enact the crime, in order to get an idea of how quickly it could have been done.'

'But why are they running in and out of the side door, when we know that the murderer came from outside and in through the French windows?' I asked.

'There's only one reason that I can think of,' replied Angela.

At that moment, realization dawned upon the rest of us and we stared at each other in consternation.

'They must suspect that someone in the house did it!' said Sylvia.

Angela nodded.

'Yes,' she said simply.

Bobs gave a great guffaw.

'But that's absurd!' he said.

'Is it?' said Angela.

'Of course it is! Quite apart from the fact that none of us had any motive to kill him, there simply wouldn't have been time. Remember what Jameson said: the murder must have taken place between a quarter to eleven and half-past one. But the outside doors were all locked at eleven o'clock. That leaves only fifteen minutes in which to do it. And if you remember, during that time we were all together in the drawing-room.'

'Not all the time,' observed Angela. 'I think several people went out—including you, Bobs.'

'Did I?' asked Bobs in surprise. 'I say, now you mention it, I believe I did. I'd completely forgotten about it. Still,' he went on, 'I don't see how there would be time to run halfway round the house, do the deed, arrange the body and return to the drawing-room without being suspected.'

'Well, let us hope that the police agree with you,' said Angela. 'Otherwise we may be in for rather a sticky time of it.'

'But why should any of us want to kill poor Neville?' said Sylvia. 'No, I won't believe it.'

'Look,' I said. 'Here comes Jameson now.'

It was indeed the inspector, striding purposefully towards us.

'Hallo, Jameson,' said Bobs, as he approached. 'We've been watching your little show here. You can't fool us. We know what you're up to. Tell me, which of us do you think did it? For my part, I don't like the look of that old butler at all. He has an evil glint in his eye and I shouldn't trust him an inch if I were you.'

'Bobs!' exclaimed Sylvia.

'Or what about Gale?' continued Bobs, unabashed. 'The ones who wouldn't say "boo" to a goose are always the ones you have to watch out for. They plod along meekly year after year, then one day the worm turns and woe betide anyone who gets in his way.'

'I'm obliged to you for your deductions, Mr. Buckley,' said the inspector politely. 'We will, of course, be considering all possibilities.'

'Bravo!' said the irrepressible Bobs. 'And now, perhaps, you will tell us what conclusions you have reached. Judging by your little show just now, you are presumably including the members of the household in your list of suspicious characters.'

The inspector smiled non-committally.

'I should not be doing my duty if I neglected any avenue of inquiry,' he said but did not elaborate further.

'Is there anything we can do to convince you that none of us had anything to do with it?' asked Sylvia.

'Why, yes, Miss Buckley, there is. That is why I am here. I am trying to get an idea of the movements of everybody in the house between the times of a quarter to eleven and eleven o'clock on Friday night.'

'Aha! I knew it!' said Bobs. 'We can tell you our own movements but not those of the servants, of course.'

'One of my men is speaking to them this afternoon,' said Inspector Jameson. 'But as for the guests—let me see, I understand that you were dancing and playing games together until a quarter to eleven. What about after that?'

I cast my mind back and tried to think. I couldn't remember much, apart from the quarrel between Joan and Gwen MacMurray.

Sylvia was the first to speak.

'It was rather an odd evening,' she said, considering. 'We were all very flat to start with, I don't quite know why. Then Rosamund came in and livened things up. She's always been very good at that. But after we had finished playing Consequences, things sort of deflated again. Then Joan and Gwen had a row about something or other and after that nobody felt much like staying up late. Most people went to bed soon afterwards.'

'At what time did the quarrel occur?' asked the inspector.

'It was just after eleven o'clock,' I said. 'I remember looking at my watch afterwards and thinking how tired I was even though it was quite early.'

'Very good,' said Jameson, consulting his notebook. 'Let me see. At a quarter to eleven you, Mr. Knox, and Lady Strickland spoke to Sir Neville through the study door. You then returned to the drawing-room.'

I assented.

'Between that time and the quarrel between Miss Havelock and Mrs. MacMurray, did any guests leave the drawing-room?'

'Oh yes, several,' said Sylvia.

'Myself included,' said Bobs. 'In fact, I missed the quarrel to which you refer altogether. I'm rather sorry about that—it sounds as though it was jolly good fun.'

'May I ask where you went?'

'I certainly didn't go and bash poor old Neville on the head, if that's what you're driving at,' replied Bobs. 'No, as a matter of fact, I went into the billiard room and practised one or two shots.'

'Who else left the drawing-room?'

'Let me think,' said Sylvia. 'Joan went out to get a book and came back. Mr. Gale went out too but didn't come back. He said he had to finish some work or something.'

'How long was Miss Havelock absent?'

'Not long. Perhaps ten or fifteen minutes.'

'Did anyone else leave?'

'I don't think so.'

Jameson made a note.

'Thank you,' he said. 'You've all been very helpful.'

Before we could ask him any questions he excused himself and went off.

'Damn,' said Bobs, as we watched him depart. 'I wanted to ask him whether they have timed the deed at less than quarter of an hour. If it took them longer then that lets us all out, of course.'

'Surely it must have taken longer than that,' said Sylvia. 'By the way, did you notice that he didn't once ask what the row between Joan and Gwen was about?'

'Perhaps he didn't think it was important,' said Angela.

'He strikes me as rather an intelligent fellow,' I said. 'Not at all like the policemen one reads about in books.'

'Then we shall all have to watch our step,' said Bobs lightly.

Chapter Eleven

I N THE HALL I met Rosamund. She brightened when she saw me and took my hand.

'I'm so glad it's you,' she said. 'Come with me to the morning-room. The handsome inspector wants to speak to Mr. Pomfrey and me about Neville's will and I'm frightened he will clap me in irons immediately and carry me off.'

'I don't think you need worry about that,' I said, 'but of course I'll come with you if you like. Won't old Pomfrey kick up a fuss, though?'

'He can fuss all he likes but I simply must have a friend with me and I know I can depend on you, Charles,' she replied.

I felt more pleased than I could say that Rosamund still considered me such a close friend. With my heart beating hard in my chest, I smiled warmly down at her. She smiled back and led me into the morning-room, where the inspector and Mr. Pomfrey were waiting.

Mr. Pomfrey was indeed unwilling to talk about Sir Neville's will in my presence but Rosamund bore down every opposition and the little solicitor was reluctantly forced to accept her wishes.

'Very well, what is it you wish to know, inspector?' he asked.

'I should like you to tell me how Sir Neville has disposed of his estate,' replied Inspector Jameson.

'Is it necessary for you to know that? I thought I understood that the murderer or murderers had entered the house from outside.'

'We have not yet established for certain how the crime was committed,' said the inspector cautiously. 'The only thing we do know at present is that a crime *was* committed, so I am required to conduct as thorough an inquiry as possible. Motive is an important factor, although it can never be conclusive, of course. That is why I ask you about the will.'

The solicitor raised his eyebrows in surprise, then leaned back in his chair and placed the tips of his fingers together.

'I see.' He considered for a moment. 'The situation is a little complicated but I shall do my best to explain. Sir Neville Strickland's will, as it stands, is fairly straightforward. There are a few minor bequests and charities, of course but there are only two main beneficiaries: Hugh MacMurray, who inherits ten thousand pounds, and Lady Strickland, who inherits the rest of Sir Neville's money—something in the region of thirty-five thousand. She also inherits the Sissingham estate but has only a life interest in it, the marriage having been without issue.'

'And who will get Sissingham when she dies?' asked the inspector.

'It reverts to Mr. MacMurray,' replied Mr. Pomfrey.

'What about Miss Havelock? Does she inherit anything?'

'No. She has an inheritance of her own, which is currently held in trust for her. She will receive that when she reaches the age of twenty-five.'

'That all seems simple enough,' said Jameson, 'and yet you said the situation was complicated. Is there something else?'

Mr. Pomfrey coughed.

'What I have just said refers to Sir Neville's will *as it stands*. However, I feel I must inform you that that was not what Sir Neville himself intended.'

The inspector paused in his writing.

'Indeed?' he said.

The solicitor coughed again.

'Yes. Sir Neville summoned me to Sissingham on Friday with regard to a new will. His wishes had changed and he wanted me to draw up a new document as soon as possible.'

'And what were the terms of the new will?'

'Under the new will, Lady Strickland would have received all Sir Neville's money and Hugh MacMurray nothing.'

'He would still have inherited Sissingham though?'

'Yes but not until after the death of Lady Strickland.'

'And Sir Neville died before the new will could be drawn up and signed. The old will stands, in other words.'

'That is so,' replied Mr. Pomfrey.

I was astonished. So what Joan had overheard was true! Sir Neville had indeed been planning to write his cousin out of his will. That would have been a huge blow to the MacMurrays. Of course, they would have Sissingham to look forward to but Rosamund would probably live for many years yet and from all I had heard, they were desperately in need of funds now. Sir Neville's death had occurred just in time for them, it seemed.

'Were you aware of the new will, Lady Strickland?' asked Inspector Jameson.

'No, not at all,' said Rosamund, who indeed had looked as surprised as anyone at the news.

'Have you any idea why Sir Neville might have decided to write his cousin out of his will?'

'I'm afraid not. I do know that Neville disapproved rather of Hugh's life in town—they run with a very fast set, you know and I gather that Hugh has not always behaved quite as he ought but I don't know of any particular reason why Neville should have taken against him so.'

The inspector addressed the solicitor once again.

'To your knowledge, was Mr. MacMurray aware of the fact that he was about to be disinherited?'

'Of that, I have no idea,' said Mr. Pomfrey primly.

I hesitated. Should I tell the inspector about the conversation Joan had overheard outside the library? I was undecided but Jameson saw my expression and took matters out of my hands.

'Mr. Knox, I think perhaps you have something to tell me,' he said gently.

I grimaced but the damage was done. Reluctantly, I related the story that Joan had told me.

'This is all hearsay, of course,' I said. 'You will have to ask Miss Havelock herself. Or better still, Hugh MacMurray.'

'Thank you Mr. Knox, I shall,' said Inspector Jameson. He made as if to rise but checked himself. 'Ah yes,' he said. 'I almost forgot. Lady Strickland, as you know there is some doubt as to how the murderer entered and left the study on the night of your husband's death. Rogers the butler tells me that the spare key with which he gained access to the study yesterday was certainly locked safely away in a drawer in his own room, and so can be eliminated from our inquiries. However, he says that there is a second set of keys to the house, which are kept locked in a drawer in Sir Neville's desk. Were you aware of their existence?'

Rosamund looked distractedly at him, as though not quite understanding the question.

'Yes,' she replied at last. 'Yes, I believe there are. I'd forgotten about them. Is it important?'

'Perhaps not. Who had the key to the desk drawer?'

'Why, Neville, I suppose.'

'Was there only one key?'

'I really have no idea. I imagine so. Have you asked Rogers?'

'Rogers says that Sir Neville kept the only key to the drawer in his pocket. He is not aware of the existence of another key.'

'Well, then, I dare say he's right,' said Rosamund. 'But what has all this to do with anything? If the house keys are locked in the drawer and Neville had the drawer key in his pocket, then that's that.' She spoke with finality.

'As you say, that's that,' agreed Jameson. 'A key was indeed found in Sir Neville's pocket. I have sent for it and we shall try it in the drawer when it arrives. If the house keys are in the drawer, then they can be disregarded too.'

He thanked us all and went out.

I wondered what he meant by his questions. Presumably the second bunch of house keys was locked safely away, in which case it was irrelevant. It seemed to me that the inspector was making things unnecessarily complicated. I supposed, however, that he had to be as thorough as possible in his investigation.

My mind turned to the will. It certainly looked as though Hugh MacMurray had had a strong motive for killing Sir Neville, although since he had been present in the drawing-room during the fatal quarter of an hour, I could not see how he could possibly have done it. In fact, the only people who could conceivably have done it in the time, having been out of the room during those fifteen minutes, were Bobs, Simon Gale and Joan Havelock. The idea of Bobs or Joan doing it was frankly ridiculous. I was less sure about Gale but on further reflection I could see no reason why he should have done it; after all, he had a comfortable berth here, with a kind employer. He had nothing to gain from Sir Neville's death and everything to lose. No, the more I considered it, the more firmly convinced I became that the police were barking up the wrong tree. It must have been someone from outside.

I left Rosamund with Mr. Pomfrey and went into the conservatory, where I found Sylvia staring absently out of the window. She turned as I entered.

'There you are,' she said. 'I wondered where you had got to.'

'Rosamund wanted me to come and hear what Mr. Pomfrey had to say about Sir Neville's will.' I said it as carelessly as possible but her eyes narrowed and she looked at me suspiciously.

'That sounds very cosy,' was all she said, however.

Faced with such a seeming lack of interest, I prepared to leave the room. Sylvia relented.

'Don't leave me in suspense!' she exclaimed. 'What did he say?'

I struggled briefly. I was certain that Mr. Pomfrey would be deeply discomposed at the thought of my spreading the news about Sir Neville's intention to disinherit his cousin. On the other hand, Rosamund had not actually said that I must not tell. The temptation to indiscretion won the day and I related all that had been said in the morning-room. Sylvia listened, wide-eyed.

'Gracious!' she said. 'If it *was* Hugh with Neville outside the library the other day, then that gives him a very strong motive for murder.'

Angela entered the room as Sylvia spoke and heard the last part of the sentence.

'Am I intruding?' she asked.

'No, not at all, listen to this,' Sylvia replied eagerly, and repeated the story. I was somewhat concerned about the news spreading so fast but had to admit that if the cat had been well and truly let out of the bag then it was my own fault.

Angela absorbed the information in silence for a moment.

'That certainly looks bad for Hugh as far as motive is concerned,' she said at last, 'but I still don't see how he could possibly have done it. He was in the drawing-room with the rest of us during the period in question.'

'But what if the murder didn't take place during that period?' I said. 'According to Inspector Jameson, it could have been committed at any time between a quarter to eleven and half-past one, if the medical evidence is to be believed.'

'Yes but if it happened after eleven o'clock, then it means that it couldn't have been done by anybody in the house—well, none of the guests, at any rate,' said Angela. 'We have two possibilities: one, that the murder was committed by an intruder from outside, in which case it might have taken place at any time during those three hours or so, since he must have entered through the French windows; two, that it was committed by somebody inside the house, in which case it must have taken place after a quarter to eleven, when you and Rosamund spoke to Neville, and before eleven, when Rogers locked the house up. After eleven o'clock it wouldn't have been possible for any of us to leave the house and enter the study from outside. Unless, of course—' she narrowed her eyes for a moment, as though considering a new idea. 'It's interesting what you say about that second set of keys, but since they stayed locked up in Neville's desk drawer I suppose there's nothing doing there.'

'What about the servants?' I said.

'It's possible but the same facts apply,' replied Angela. 'The house was locked up at eleven with everyone inside it, although I suppose it's just barely possible that one of them left the house before that time and returned when the doors were unlocked the next morning. I imagine the police have occupied themselves with that inquiry, however.'

Sylvia was frowning.

'Wait!' she said. 'Why are we assuming that the murderer entered through the French windows? Let's say that someone from the house did do it. Why couldn't he have entered the study through the door? Perhaps Neville simply let him in.'

'Perhaps,' said Angela, considering. 'It certainly might have happened that way but it would still have to have been between a quarter to eleven and eleven o'clock. When Neville was found, the study door had been locked from the inside, which means that the murderer would have had to leave through the French windows and come back in another way, perhaps through the side door, perhaps some other way that we haven't thought of yet.'

'And it also means that the only people who could have done it are still Bobs, Joan and Simon Gale,' said Sylvia. 'Oh, it's too absurd for words! It *must* have been an intruder from outside.'

Angela shook her head.

'I have the feeling that the police are coming to a rather different conclusion,' she said seriously. 'That is what I came in to tell you. A few minutes ago I spoke to Joan, who has an enviable knack for getting information out of the servants. It appears that the police have not been able to find any sign that the crime was an "outside job", as I believe it is called. They are inclined to believe that it was committed by someone inside the house.'

'Then they're wrong,' said Sylvia stoutly, 'or they've got all their times wrong.'

'I must say I agree,' I said. 'The fact that there is no evidence for an intruder doesn't necessarily prove it was done by one of the household. Perhaps the intruder didn't leave any evidence.'

'It would have been difficult for him not to. It's been very muddy since the rain on Friday,' Angela observed.

'Yes, but we have all been tramping about the grounds since then. Any tracks could easily have been erased. And if someone from inside did it, wouldn't he have left footprints?'

'I don't think he would. Remember that the terrace runs right round the house. There would have been no need for him to get his shoes dirty at all,' replied Angela.

'Even assuming it was an inside job, I don't see how it could have been done in those fifteen minutes,' said Sylvia, thinking. 'It doesn't make sense. And the very idea of Bobs or Joan doing it is ridiculous!'

'But what about Gale?' I said. 'He went out of the room and didn't come back. He says he finished some work and then went to bed but do we have any evidence of that?'

We fell silent, considering Simon Gale as a suspect.

'He *could* have done it, I suppose,' I said at last. 'But what about a motive? He seems rather a nervous type but he told me he was very happy here. What reason could he have for killing Sir Neville?'

As soon as I said it, however, my mind jumped back to the row between Gwen and Joan on the night Sir Neville died. What was it that Gwen had said? Something about Joan mooning about after Gale. I had dismissed the accusation as mere spite but what if it were true? And what if Joan's feelings were returned? Perhaps there was an actual understanding between them. I wondered how Sir Neville would react to the news.

'Do you think there was anything in what Gwen said the other night about Joan and Gale?' I asked tentatively.

The other two looked surprised.

'You mean about Joan being in love with Simon?' said Sylvia. 'I don't know. I thought it was just Gwen being spiteful. Joan always was a bit of a dark horse, though, and I suppose Simon Gale does rather seem like the kind of lost cause that would attract someone like her. Is it important?'

'That depends,' I replied. 'I was just wondering whether Sir Neville would have approved of an engagement between them.'

'Oh, I see,' said Sylvia. 'You're picturing Neville as the stern guardian, throwing Simon out of the house and locking Joan up so she can never see him again. But really, you've got it all wrong. Neville simply wasn't that sort. I don't suppose he would have been too pleased if in fact they *are* engaged, but I can't see him being all Victorian about it either. No, that won't do as a motive for murder, Charles.'

'Well, you knew Sir Neville better than I,' I said, reluctantly abandoning my theory. 'I suppose it does seem rather far-fetched.'

'Look at us,' said Angela ruefully. 'Here we are, wondering whether someone we know has committed murder simply because he seems the least unlikely suspect out of a group of three unlikely suspects. It's rather unfair on poor Mr. Gale. I think we ought to stop inventing theories.'

'But—' I began and stopped as Joan herself entered the conservatory. Luckily, she did not notice our sheepish expressions but burst out:

'Can't someone stop that dreadful inspector? He is turning the house completely upside-down and now he's upset Simon and I can't find him anywhere!'

CHAPTER TWELVE

WHAT DO YOU mean, he's upset Simon?' asked Angela.
'Oh, he just kept on asking him questions about
where he was and what he was doing during those fifteen minutes,' said Joan, throwing her hands up in despair. 'Just because
he is conscientious about doing his work properly, the police
seem to think he must be a murderer! It's not his fault if he was
out of the room when Neville was k—killed. And now I don't
know where he's gone and I'm so afraid he might have done
something silly. He's not strong. He can't cope with this sort of
thing.'

She burst into tears as she spoke. Angela went to comfort
her.

'Don't cry, darling,' she said. 'He wouldn't do anything silly,
I'm sure.'

'But I've looked all over the house!' wailed Joan.

'He's probably gone out for a walk in the grounds,' said Sylvia reasonably. 'That's what I should do if someone had upset
me and I wanted to cool down.'

'Do you really think so?' said Joan. 'I couldn't see him from any of the upstairs windows. But perhaps you're right.'

'What exactly did he say?' I asked.

'Oh, I don't know, he just muttered something about getting away and hurried off. I should have followed him. I shall never forgive myself if anything happens to him.'

'I'm sure there's no need to worry,' said Angela soothingly. 'Of course it is difficult for all of us at the moment but the police have to do their job. Simon probably just wanted to get away from the pressure for a while. I'm sure he will turn up for tea.'

'I dare say you're right,' said Joan, dabbing her eyes with a handkerchief. 'But I can't help worrying.'

But Simon Gale did not turn up to tea, or to dinner either. It was soon discovered that he had taken Sir Neville's car and had last been seen heading for the nearest town.

'Well, that's that, then,' said Bobs, when he heard that Gale had gone missing. 'Nice of him to save us the bother of a police investigation but he could have had the decency to stay here and face up to it.'

Indeed, most of the party seemed to take it for granted that Gale's disappearance was tantamount to a confession of murder, even though he had no apparent motive. I supposed that as a nervous type, he had experienced some kind of temporary disorder of the brain that had caused him to lash out and kill his employer. Remembering Gale's pale face as we debated the Mason case at dinner, I wondered whether the subject had struck too close to home: whether, in fact, he had known of his weakness and his own liability to resort to violence.

The police immediately instituted a search for the missing man, scouring the countryside for any trace of him and in the meantime, I think the rest of us, with the possible exception of Joan, felt something of a sense of relief that the matter had been resolved so rapidly.

I mentioned this to Angela Marchmont.

'Yes,' she said. 'It does look rather damning for Mr. Gale— the fact that he has run off, I mean.'

'But you are not convinced by the other evidence?'

'That's just it,' she replied. 'There is no other evidence—no positive evidence, anyway. Just the fact that we don't know where he was or what he was doing in those fifteen minutes.'

'Surely that's enough, if everybody else has been eliminated from the inquiry?'

'Perhaps. It may be absurd of me, Mr. Knox but I can't seem to shake off the feeling that we have been—oh, what is the word I'm looking for?'

'But what other solution could there be?'

'I don't know,' she said. 'There's no reason for me to doubt anything I've heard up to now and yet—'

'And yet what?'

She shook herself.

'Misdirected,' she said firmly. 'That's the word I was thinking of. We have been misdirected. Now, I must think.'

Just then, we were interrupted by Rosamund, who drew me away from Angela as she had a request to make.

'I simply can't bear the idea of being all alone in this house at the moment,' she said. 'I am going to ask all my guests to stay with me for another few days, to keep me company. You *will* stay, won't you Charles?' She looked at me beseechingly.

I had in fact been considering how best to withdraw discreetly, on the assumption that I could not possibly be wanted at such a time and should only be in the way, so the question came as something of a surprise.

'Of course I will stay, if that is what you want,' I said. 'But are you sure that I won't be more of a hindrance than a help? I should have thought that you would prefer not to have the distraction of a party of guests just now.'

'Oh but a party of guests is just what I need, to keep my mind off things,' she said eagerly. 'Please, Charles, *do* say you'll stay.'

Naturally I could not refuse such a request, especially when Rosamund made such a particular point of it. I acceded and she took my hand and thanked me warmly.

'Now, you must take a walk with me,' she said. 'I badly need some fresh air and I've had no opportunity to speak to you in the last day or two, although I suppose that's hardly surprising, given the circumstances.'

I looked up sharply at her last words, which sounded suddenly forlorn. Dear Rosamund, I thought. She had borne up bravely so far like a true Englishwoman, but how long would it last?

Everyone agreed to remain at Sissingham for the present—indeed, I was glad to do so, for I had no other engagements and it was a pleasure to feel that I could be of service to Rosamund in any way. But it was impossible to pretend that the events of the previous days had not occurred and we all struggled to find things to do that would not be thought unseemly.

Inspector Jameson, meanwhile, had been drawn into the hunt and had departed from the house, leaving behind him a constable, who was laboriously establishing the movements of the servants. We had been told that the inquest into Sir Neville's death would almost certainly be adjourned while the search for Simon Gale continued.

'That will no doubt be a great disappointment to the local populace,' observed Bobs, who was reading a newspaper as we all sat at the breakfast table.

'What do you mean?' I said.

'Look,' he said and passed me the paper. I looked and my heart leapt into my mouth.

'"Suspicious Death at Country Estate",' I read. 'What does it mean?'

'It means, old chap, that the press have got hold of the story. I suppose we can expect every penny rag in the land to send its finest sleuth-hounds down here shortly.'

'Oh, I do hope not,' said Rosamund.

I read on. It was the usual type of sensational news story, a mixture of truths, half-truths and inventions, written by somebody who had evidently never been to Sissingham or met any of the parties concerned. It dwelt heavily on the disappearance of Simon Gale.

'The whole country will be looking out for Gale now,' said Bobs. 'I don't think much of his chances.'

'"Inspector Jameson of Scotland Yard and his men have collected several clues,"' I read, '"and it is to be hoped that the culprit will be apprehended very soon."'

'Look, Rosamund, they have dug up a photograph of you,' said Joan, who had been reading over my shoulder. 'Wherever did they get it? And isn't that you, Bobs?'

'Oh yes,' said Bobs carelessly. 'I don't remember where it was taken. Somewhere abroad, by the looks of it.'

I looked at the photograph, which showed a group of fashionable people standing in the sunshine outside what looked like a large and elegant hotel. Rosamund was one of them and there too, grinning foolishly, was Bobs.

'"Lady Strickland and friends in Mentone last year,"' I read.

'You didn't tell me you went to Mentone last year, Bobs,' said Sylvia.

'Surely you can't expect me to inform you of everything I do,' replied her brother. 'I flit hither and thither like a butterfly, bestowing the bounty of my great beauty and wisdom upon all whom I meet. I have no time for the niceties by which lesser beings must abide. Don't I look dashing in tennis whites?' He stretched his arms out painfully. 'I say, I shall have to get back into condition before I play again. My arms are aching badly today and all I did was move those two heavy plants of Joan's yesterday. All this wallowing in the lap of luxury has turned me into a shadow, a mere shadow.'

I saw Mrs. Marchmont look sharply at him and then frown, as though trying to remember something.

'Neville isn't in the picture. Where was he that day, I wonder,' said Joan.

'Somewhere about, I expect,' said Bobs. 'I remember it was fearfully hot.'

'Never mind that,' said Rosamund. 'A more important question is what on earth possessed me to wear that awful hat?'

As they laughed over the photograph, Rogers appeared and announced the return of Inspector Jameson, who wished to speak to Lady Strickland privately.

'Oh,' said Rosamund, 'perhaps he has some news about Simon.'

She went out but returned a few minutes later.

'What did he want? Has Simon been found?' asked Joan immediately.

'No, he hasn't been found,' said Rosamund. I noticed she looked rather pale. 'But they're very anxious to find him as soon as possible. You see, it turns out that he has an alibi. Two servants saw him at different times during that fifteen-minute period, so it would have been impossible for him to have committed the murder in the time.'

We all looked at each other.

'Are you saying that Simon is innocent?' said Gwen. 'I don't believe it! Why, if he is innocent, then that means someone else must have done it.'

'Bravo,' said Bobs.

'But none of us did it, did we?' insisted Gwen. 'So it must have been Simon.'

'Oh, don't be ridiculous,' snapped Joan. It looked as though another row was about to start but Rosamund forestalled it.

'Hugh,' she said. 'Inspector Jameson would like to speak to you in the morning-room.'

MacMurray's shocked expression was almost comical.

'Me? What does he want to see me for?'

'He didn't say,' said Rosamund.

As he went out, I glanced over at Sylvia and saw her look-ing at me. She raised her eyebrows. Now that Gale had been cleared, it looked as though Hugh MacMurray was the next in line to be suspected and there was no need to look very far for a motive. Ten thousand pounds would have been a big enough temptation at any time but presumably the MacMur-rays could have afforded to wait, being regular beneficiaries of Sir Neville's generous hospitality. However, Sir Neville's threat to change his will would have been a powerful spur to action, especially once Mr. Pomfrey had arrived and the MacMurrays could see that Sir Neville really did mean what he said. Per-haps uncharitably, I did not imagine for a second that Hugh MacMurray would have murdered Sir Neville without encour-agement, even goading, from his wife. He didn't seem to me to have the guts, but I had no doubt that Gwen was quite capable of murdering anybody who stood in her way. The main stum-bling-block, of course, was the fact that they had both been in the drawing-room during the time in question.

I got up and left the room. At the bottom of the stairs I paused and glanced down the passage to my left. A servant was entering the study. I went into the library, where I found a policeman examining the window. He nodded at me affably and went out. A few minutes later, I found him in my room, looking at the window there too. He excused himself and said something about routine inquiries.

'Now why is he looking at all the windows, I wonder?' I said to myself, staring down the passage at him as he left.

'Hallo,' said Angela Marchmont, who was just coming out of her own room. 'Has the policeman been examining your window too? I wondered when it would occur to them.'

'I don't see why,' I said.

'Don't you see? It's because of that famous quarter of an hour. The police have finally come to the conclusion that it is just a red herring and that the crime could equally have happened later on, after eleven o'clock.'

'But how? I don't understand.'

Angela explained.

'Well, the only people who were out of the drawing-room during the fatal fifteen minutes were Mr. Gale, Bobs and Joan. Mr. Gale has an alibi, Joan was absent for only a few minutes and it has now emerged that Bobs was playing billiards with one of the servants but kept quiet about it because he didn't want to get the man into trouble. There wasn't time for any of them to kill Neville and arrange the scene.'

'Then it must have been done by an outsider, as we originally thought!' I said.

'I don't think the police are looking at it like that. They have made very thorough inquiries. This is a very quiet place and no stranger has been seen in the area for weeks. I suppose until they find clear evidence that it was an outside job—evidence that has been lacking up to now—they will continue to work on the theory that the crime was committed by somebody in the house, some time between a quarter to eleven and half-past one. But since the outside doors were locked at eleven o'clock, anyone who wanted to get into Neville's study through the French windows after that time would presumably have to leave the house through a window.'

'Not an upstairs window, surely,' I said.

'No,' agreed Angela. 'I had a look myself yesterday and there are no handy creepers to shin down, or anything like that. Whoever it was would have had to sneak downstairs after everybody was asleep and get out through a downstairs window—although I think it's more likely that he was simply let in through the study door by Neville himself and just returned that way.

'But which window was it?'

'I don't know. Perhaps the police will find that none of them are passable, in which case we are back where we started.'

'I must say, it's looking rather bad for MacMurray,' I said. 'If all this is true, then he had not only an opportunity but also a thumping great motive.'

'Yes,' said Angela. 'But it also means that we are all back in the picture, including Mr. Gale.'

'Is this what you meant when you said we had been misdirected?'

'Partly. Yes, I did think that the famous quarter of an hour might after all come to mean nothing. It seemed such a short time in which to commit a murder and make it look like an accident, especially if the whole affair was unpremeditated.'

'Do you think it *was* unpremeditated, then?'

'I don't see how it could have been anything else. The staging of the scene was so clumsily and amateurishly done that it gives every indication of having been carried out in a tearing hurry and without any forethought. Even we spotted almost immediately that there was something odd about the position of Neville's body.'

'But if, as you say, it was done in a tearing hurry, why couldn't it have been done in the time? Surely to enter the study, bang Sir Neville on the head and move his body and a few other things around couldn't have taken long.'

'First of all, we now know that if it was done during that period, then it must have taken fifteen minutes or less, given that nobody was out of sight for more than that time. But even more importantly, if we are assuming that the crime was unpremeditated, then it would be highly unlikely for the killer to have entered the room and knocked Neville out immediately, without preliminaries. Try and think about it from the murderer's point of view. He enters the room with a view to talking to Neville about something, not hitting him on the head. There must be some conversation at least, some altercation, before he is driven to murder and that would take several minutes at least.'

'Not necessarily. If MacMurray is indeed the killer, then he had a motive before he even entered the room. He may well have gone in there with murder in mind and dispatched the business immediately.' Another idea suddenly came to me. 'And why, if the thing was not planned in advance, were the French windows left open to allow the killer to enter?'

'We don't know they were, yet,' replied Angela. 'As I said, he may have gone in through the study door and merely left that way, then climbed back in through a window.'

'How did he know to leave the window open then, if he was not intending to kill?'

'I don't know,' said Angela. 'There are lots of things that don't add up about this business. But one thing we can say for certain is that if Hugh is the one responsible, then he must have done it after eleven o'clock, as he was in the drawing-room with the rest of us for most of the evening. It's just that somehow I can't see Hugh as a murderer.'

'It all makes perfect sense to me. I can see it all now. This is what I think happened: after everyone else has gone to bed MacMurray, desperate to keep his inheritance and get back into Sir Neville's good books, creeps downstairs and knocks on the study door with a view to pleading his case. After he has been admitted, things go badly wrong, they have a row, MacMurray kills Sir Neville and arranges the body, then leaves through the French windows.'

'But how did he know Neville would be there, if everyone had gone to bed?' said Angela. 'And how did he get back into the house?'

I thought.

'In that case, it *must* have been premeditated. He went downstairs with murder in mind, making sure first that he would be able to lock the study door behind him, leave through the French windows and come back into the house through a window. It's the only possible way. And I wonder,' I continued, 'whether Gwen mightn't have been part of the whole plot. She started the row with Joan, if you remember. Perhaps that was deliberately cooked up between them, in order to drive everybody to bed early. I don't know how they could be so sure that Sir Neville would still be up, though. That's the only flaw I can think of.'

'What you say is quite plausible,' admitted Angela. 'But somehow I'm not convinced by it. I think there is something we have missed but I can't quite put my finger on it.'

We went downstairs together and parted in the hall. I stood for a moment to let the servant whom I had seen going into the study earlier pass me, then went down the passage and into the room where Sir Neville had died. I looked about me. Nothing about the place gave any suggestion of the violent event that had taken place there only a few days earlier. I moved over to the desk and tried one of the drawers, then jumped violently as someone coughed softly behind me. I swung round.

'Were you perhaps looking for this?' said Inspector Jameson.

Chapter Thirteen

THE INSPECTOR HELD out a telegram.

'Where did you get that?' I asked, when I finally found my voice.

'From that drawer,' he replied.

'You shouldn't look through people's private things,' I said, rather lamely.

He gave a small smile.

'I'm afraid it is a regrettable part of my job,' he said.

'I gather you've read it.'

'Yes.'

'Then it contains all the information you require and I have no more to say on the matter,' I said with emphasis and made as if to leave.

'Oh, come now, Mr. Knox,' said Jameson. 'I have here in my hand a telegram from Sir Neville's agent in South Africa, bringing to Sir Neville's attention the fact that, three years ago, a Mr. Charles Knox was tried for the murder of one Franklin

Watson of Johannesburg. I myself am investigating a murder, so naturally this fact is of great interest to me.'

'As you will see from the telegram, I was tried and *acquitted*,' I said stiffly.

'Suppose you tell me about it. Shall we sit down?'

I sat.

'Very well, since it seems I have no choice,' I said. 'What is it you wish to know?'

'First of all, who was Franklin Watson?'

'He was my business partner. It is to him that I owe all my good fortune in the mining business. I had gone out to South Africa to try my hand at farming and was making a pretty poor fist of it when I met old Frank. He had been out there for years and had finally struck gold but needed a partner to help him exploit it. He chose me. I shall always be grateful to him for that.'

'How did he die?'

'He was found one morning in his hotel room, lying on his bed with his head staved in. One hand was clutching a half-empty bottle of whisky.' As soon as I said it, I bit my tongue. 'But the circumstances were quite different in this case,' I went on hurriedly. 'Frank liked his drink—liked it rather too much. If he had managed to lay off the stuff, then he wouldn't have needed an able-bodied partner to help him in the business. He was a very capable man when sober. The whisky was certainly his; it wasn't just spilt around to lay a false scent. I don't know who killed him. I wish I did. The mining business attracts a lot of transients and a rich man a lot of enemies and it could have been any one of them.'

'Then why did the police arrest *you*?'

I shifted uncomfortably. Would those horrible events of three years ago continue to haunt me for the rest of my life?

'We had had a row the night before and had been overheard by several people. One man swore in court that he had heard me threatening to kill Frank: it's not true, I tell you. Every one of those witnesses was a drunkard and a wastrel. The whole thing was a trumped-up charge against me, anybody could see that. The jury certainly did.'

I realized I was becoming heated and relapsed into moody silence.

'I see,' said Inspector Jameson. 'So you were acquitted. Now we come to the events of the past few days. This is not the first time you have attempted to enter the study since Sir Neville's death, my men tell me, so, unless there is something else we have missed in our searches I think we can safely assume that you knew the telegram was here and were trying to get it back before we found it and jumped to conclusions. I therefore deduce that Sir Neville had spoken to you about it. Would you be so kind as to tell me the details of that conversation?'

'There's not much to tell. I returned home to England a little over a month ago and had begun informal negotiations with Sir Neville and Bobs—Mr. Buckley's father, Lord Haverford, about some prospecting rights back in Jo'burg. Sir Neville must have made inquiries of his agent about me and the agent telegraphed back the reply you have in your hand. He asked me directly whether it was true that I had been tried for murder and I hope I convinced him that I was an innocent man unjustly accused.'

'Is that all? He did not, for example, threaten to expose you to your friends? Pardon me, but some people might take a dim view of your past—er—misfortunes.'

'No, he did not,' I replied firmly. 'On the contrary, he shook my hand and said that as he had no reason to doubt my word he would keep the matter quiet for my sake.'

'Did that include keeping the matter from Lord Haverford?'

'That is how I understood it, yes.'

'Mr. Knox, did you kill Sir Neville Strickland?'

'No, I did not kill him. If I had, then I should have taken good care to remove that telegram.'

'Is there anything at all you can tell me that might shed light on Sir Neville's murder?'

I hesitated.

'I'm not sure,' I replied at last. 'During our conversation, Sir Neville said that somebody had been scheming against him, or something of the sort. At first I thought he must be talking about me, as he shortly afterwards showed me the telegram, but the more I think about it, the more convinced I am that he was referring to someone else. The murder trial is a shameful episode in my past—I admit it—and I have kept very quiet about it as you know, but I could hardly be accused of scheming against him.'

'That's very interesting,' said Jameson. 'Can you remember his exact words?'

I thought back.

'I think he said something about troubles all coming at once and that somebody had deceived him and he was upset about it. Yes, and he certainly said that he felt he was surrounded by liars and schemers. Those were his words, if I recall correctly.'

'And you have no idea to whom he was referring?'

'None at all.'

The inspector must have detected a note of hesitation in my voice, because he said:

'Are you quite certain of that, Mr. Knox?'

I relented.

'Well, it has occurred to me since then that he might have been referring to the MacMurrays. As you know, he asked Mr. Pomfrey to come to Sissingham because he wanted to change his will and write Hugh MacMurray out of it. What reason could he have had for doing that if not the discovery of some misdeed on MacMurray's part? But that idea only occurred to me long after our conversation; I mean to say, it was not an impression I got at the time.'

'I see,' he said again.

'Is there anything else?' I asked.

'Just one thing. I would like to ask your permission for my men to have a look through your belongings.'

'My belongings?'

'Not only yours,' he corrected himself. 'I have asked all the guests the same thing. It is a matter of routine.'

'Searching for evidence?' I said. 'Well, of course it will look very suspicious if I say no, so I suppose I shall have to say yes, even if I don't like it.'

'Thank you Mr. Knox. That will be all for the present.'

I rose to go.

'Will it be necessary for you to tell anybody about what we have just been discussing?' I asked.

'I see no reason to do so at the moment. I shall be discreet as far as possible,' he replied.

I left, my mind in a turmoil. I had remained more or less composed while answering the inspector's questions but had felt deeply uncomfortable all the while. And I had not been entirely truthful when I said that Sir Neville had shaken my hand. He had made as if to do it but then had thought better of it at the last minute and covered up the movement with a cough. At that moment, I had known that he still doubted my innocence.

I returned to the drawing-room to find Gwen protesting loudly at the very idea of the police searching through her things.

'No, I tell you, I won't allow it!' she exclaimed. 'This is treating us all like common criminals, when we all know that Simon did it. Why should I let a stranger snoop through my clothes?'

'We don't know that Simon did it,' said Rosamund. 'And as you are innocent, of course the police won't find anything, will they?' she continued in her most persuasive tones. 'And that will eliminate you from their inquiries and they'll stop bothering you. Now darling, do say yes like the rest of us.'

'All right then, but I don't like it,' said Gwen sulkily.

'Where have you been?' Sylvia asked me in a low voice. 'You've missed all the fun.'

'Talking to Inspector Jameson,' I muttered. 'What happened?'

'Come outside and I'll tell you.'

It was a dull, chilly day and a dank mist hung low over the park.

'It's all looking rather bad for MacMurray,' I remarked.

'That's exactly what I was going to say,' said Sylvia eagerly.

'Why, what happened?'

'After you went out, Hugh came back looking rather dazed and before Gwen could stop him, blurted out the whole story. Apparently, the police have discovered why Neville intended to disinherit him.'

'Oh?'

'Yes,' she went on. 'It seems that a friend of Neville's took him aside one day and said did he know that Hugh had been chucked out of his club for disreputable conduct—something to do with illegal gambling, or running a book, or something. Neville did a bit of investigating on his own account and found out that it was true and confronted Hugh with the facts. Hugh admitted it, said that it had just been a harmless game among friends and promised to stick to the straight and narrow from now on. He must have lapsed back into his old ways, though, as not long afterwards the suspicion arose at another club that he was running some betting operation in concert with someone called Myerson, who is apparently the absolute end, although I've never heard of him. When Neville found out he went into fits.'

I whistled in astonishment.

'Not really? Clem Myerson? Surely you must have read about him in the newspapers? He is one of the most notorious criminals in London. He is thought to have a finger in every pie: guns, drug-running, illegal gambling and worse. Many of his gang are already behind bars, although the police have not been able to touch him—it is thought that he pays his associates handsomely to take the blame and rules over his men by a combination of persuasion and fear. He has a taste for better things, though, and is often seen mingling with some of the more disreputable elements of high society. If MacMurray has been consorting with Clem Myerson then it's no wonder that Sir Neville decided to disinherit him!'

'Goodness!' said Sylvia. 'Anyway, Hugh was accused of acting as Myerson's "inside man" in clubland, giving him access to lots of people with plenty of money.'

'If he has admitted all this, then why didn't Inspector Jameson arrest him immediately?'

'He didn't admit it. The inspector confronted him with the accusations that had been made against him and he denied them, although of course he couldn't deny that the accusations had been made. His story is that he had met Myerson a few times but knew nothing of his reputation, and that Neville had made a mistake. He is convinced that he would have been able to persuade Neville to change his mind if Neville hadn't been killed.'

'Do you think his story is true?'

She shrugged.

'Who knows? I've always thought that Hugh was a bit of an ass but harmless enough.'

'But what about the murder? He hasn't been arrested, so presumably no-one has been able to find any evidence against him.'

'No, he hasn't been arrested—yet,' she said. 'But the police are searching through all our belongings now. I wonder what they are looking for.'

I told her about the conversation I had had with Angela Marchmont earlier, about the police's new theory regarding the windows and the time at which the murder had happened.

'I expect they are examining the knees of our trousers and suchlike, for signs that someone has been clambering about the place,' I said.

'It wasn't me, anyhow,' said Sylvia. 'By the way, what did Inspector Jameson want to speak to you about?'

'Oh, he merely wanted to ask me whether I knew of any reason why someone would want to kill Sir Neville,' I said airily. 'Of course I said no.'

Sylvia turned to look at me.

'Charles, do you really think Hugh did it?' she said.

'Who else could it have been?'

She did not answer.

'He is the most obvious suspect. After all, he had the motive and the opportunity.'

'If what you say is true, then we all had the opportunity,' she said.

'But nobody else had such a strong motive, you must see that. Sir Neville was about to disinherit him, so he had to act fast.'

'We don't know that nobody else had a motive. Hugh's is just the one we know about. There are all kinds of reasons for killing someone and money is only one of them. The murderer might have acted out of—oh, I don't know—out of love, or jealousy, or fear, or even just pure hatred.'

'True but money seems to be the most obvious motive in Sir Neville's case. I think we can discount love and jealousy as reasons and I don't know who could have feared or hated him enough to kill him.'

'Well *someone* killed him.'

'Tell me, then, who do you think did it?'

'I don't know,' she said, 'but I don't like it, Charles. I hate all this sneaking around and talking in corners and looking sideways at my friends wondering which one of them is a murderer. I wish—'

'Yes?'

She said nothing for a moment, then burst out:

'I wish we'd left well alone and never gone snooping around in the study. Then Neville could have been buried decently and we could all have gone about our business as before. Nothing will ever be the same again now.'

'It wouldn't have made any difference,' I said. 'We weren't the only ones to be suspicious—it was the doctor who raised the alarm, remember, when he arrived with Mr. Pomfrey.'

'Oh, damn and blast the man, why couldn't he have kept his suspicions to himself?' she said. 'Mr. Pomfrey didn't want to say anything, I could tell. It was Dr. Carter who had to go and spoil everything.'

After my bruising interview with Inspector Jameson, I was beginning to share her feelings. At first, I had been only too keen to see the killer brought to justice and had been surprised at the reluctance to call the police displayed by Sylvia, Mrs. Marchmont and the solicitor. But of course then there was no suspicion that the crime had been committed by someone in the house. I began to see the enormity of what had happened. Sylvia was right. Nothing would ever be the same again.

Sylvia shivered.

'I'm cold,' she said. 'Let's go back inside.'

We returned to the house in silence. Sylvia looked glum— as did I, probably. Little as I liked the man, I had no wish to see Hugh MacMurray hanged for murder or his wife arrested as an accessory, but it now looked inevitable. All that was needed was some evidence, which I had no doubt the police would soon find. In fact, as it turned out, the evidence was provided by MacMurray himself.

CHAPTER FOURTEEN

W E WERE GREETED in the hall by a beaming Joan. 'Have you heard the good news?' she demanded breathlessly. 'They've found Simon! And he's all right!'

We duly expressed our surprise and satisfaction.

'Where did they find him?' asked Sylvia.

'Well, they found the car first of all, on the beach near Aldeburgh with the waves lapping around it. They thought the worst at first but it was just that the silly ass hadn't thought to leave it out of the reach of the high tide. He was found a little way away, sitting on the sand and staring out to sea. His mother lives nearby, you know, in one of those rest homes for decayed gentlewomen. I believe she's quite ga-ga now, poor old thing. That's what made them think he might be there. Anyway, he must have been having one of his nervous attacks, as they couldn't get a word out of him for hours. Poor Simon! I hope the police are being kind to him.'

I smiled and thought what a kind-hearted soul Joan was, despite her cross demeanour. She would make Gale a good wife, once this terrible business was all over and done with.

'Is he coming back here?' I asked.

'Oh yes. Rosamund insisted on it. Simon was dreadfully embarrassed about the whole thing and wanted to slink off and hide somewhere but Rosamund wouldn't hear of it. She said that Sissingham was his home and that he needed looking after. It was really very kind of her.'

I forbore to point out that Inspector Jameson was probably very keen himself for Gale to return to the house: after all, although he had an alibi for the fifteen minutes between a quarter to eleven and eleven o'clock, he was still as much under suspicion as the rest of us for the period until half-past one. Here at Sissingham, it would be much easier for the police to keep an eye on us and wait for someone to make a wrong move.

The search of our belongings had taken place and, it seemed, had drawn a blank. Certainly, nothing was removed and no-one was questioned further. Furthermore, we received hints that the police were perplexed as to how the killer had got back into the house after the murder. According to Joan, one of the servants had overheard a constable reporting that the downstairs windows were either impossible to open or too high off the ground to allow anyone to pass through them easily. I began to wonder if the crime would ever be solved, given that each time an avenue of inquiry opened up, it seemed to be closed off again immediately.

Simon Gale returned after tea, accompanied by the inspector. Rosamund had warned us all not to make a fuss or mention his escapade and we mostly succeeded, except for Hugh MacMurray who, as was only to be expected, clapped him on the back and made one or two loud remarks in dubious taste, which caused Gale to wince. He hurried off as soon as was decently possible and was reported as having gone to the study in order to arrange Sir Neville's papers and bury himself in his work.

The inspector had come for only a brief visit, he told us, to report on the progress of the case to Lady Strickland. He was preparing to depart when he suddenly paused.

'Ah,' he said. 'I almost forgot these.'

He reached into his jacket, drew out of his note-case several scraps of folded paper and placed them on a nearby table. Gwen MacMurray took one of them up.

'Why, it's our Consequences game,' she exclaimed. 'Whatever did you take these for?'

'Just part of our routine investigation,' replied Jameson. 'We've finished examining them now.'

I failed to see what clue could be gleaned from a childish game but supposed the inspector had had his reasons. Hugh MacMurray had taken a paper too and let out a loud guffaw as he read it.

'Oh I say! That's very good,' he said and reached for another one.

'Boopsie, you've already read them,' said his wife impatiently.

'No I haven't,' he replied. 'I missed the game, don't you remember? I was taking a turn on the terrace at the time. Shame, though—it sounds like it was rather a laugh, what?'

At that moment, I saw both Inspector Jameson and Angela Marchmont turn their heads towards MacMurray and regard him thoughtfully.

'Mr. MacMurray, how long were you out walking on the terrace?' asked Jameson.

'Eh, what's that?' replied MacMurray, tearing his eyes away from the paper he held in his hand. 'Oh, I don't know. Half an hour, perhaps more.'

'Oh yes,' said Rosamund. 'Charles and I met you on our way back to the drawing-room from the study, didn't we?'

I heard Angela let out a soft 'Oh!'

The inspector said nothing and went out.

Half an hour or so later he returned and asked Rosamund if she would kindly join him in the morning-room, as he had just remembered something he had meant to ask her earlier.

'Yes, certainly,' said Rosamund, surprised. She rose and they went out. A few minutes later, Rogers came in and murmured discreetly in my ear that Inspector Jameson would be pleased if I would join them. Puzzled, I went along to the morning-room at once, to find Rosamund and the inspector sitting in close conference.

'Oh, Charles,' said Rosamund, when she saw me. 'Inspector Jameson has asked me the most extraordinary question which concerns us both, so I insisted that you be present. Now, inspector,' she continued, turning to him, 'do repeat what you said. It's simply too odd for words!'

I had the feeling that this was not how the inspector would have preferred to conduct the interview but he went on politely.

'Mr. Knox,' he said. 'I have been asking Lady Strickland about the events that occurred shortly before a quarter to eleven, when she and you went to the study and attempted to persuade Sir Neville to join his guests.'

'Go on,' I said.

'Before then, I understand you were all playing at Consequences. Do you remember at what time the game began?'

'I'm afraid I don't,' I replied. 'I suggest you ask Mr. Gale that, as he seems to have a perfect memory for that kind of thing.'

'Shall we fetch him in?' said Rosamund brightly. Before the inspector could object, she rang the bell and had him summoned.

'Oh, Simon,' she said, when Gale arrived. 'The inspector is asking us questions about the night of Neville's death and I've such a frightfully bad memory that I need your help. He wants to know at what time we started playing Consequences. Do you remember?'

Gale thought for a moment.

'I think it must have been a few minutes before ten o'clock, Lady Strickland. I remember looking at my watch and thinking that I had some work to finish and that I had better start soon.'

Rosamund sat back, pleased.

'There, you see?' she said. 'I told you Simon would remember.'

'Do you remember who was in the room at the time?' asked Jameson of Gale. 'That is, who was playing?'

'Oh, we all played,' said Gale. 'Except for Mr. MacMurray, that is. He had left the room a few minutes earlier.'

'I see,' said Inspector Jameson. 'Thank you, Mr. Gale.'

'But what does it all mean?' asked Rosamund, when Gale had gone. 'Why do you want to know about what happened then? We know Neville was alive at that time, because Charles and I spoke to him, didn't we, Charles?' She turned to me, appealing for confirmation.

A dim light was beginning to dawn in my head.

'We did call to him through the door, yes,' I said carefully, with a glance at the inspector. He nodded in approval and consulted his notebook.

'On the day after Sir Neville's death,' he said, 'you, Lady Strickland, told me that you and Mr. Knox had gone to the study and spoken to Sir Neville through the closed door, in an attempt to persuade him to come and join the game. He refused, saying that he had some work to finish.' The inspector leaned forward. 'Now, I would like you to think back very carefully, both of you. Can you be absolutely certain that it was Sir Neville who spoke to you?'

'But of course!' said Rosamund. 'Who else could it have been? Charles, you heard him too.'

I shook my head.

'Truth to tell I don't think I heard anything at all. You arrived a little before me and I couldn't hear what was being said. The door is very thick, which would muffle the sound.'

Rosamund reflected.

'Yes, the sound was very muffled, but I was sure it was Neville.'

'Could it have been Mr. MacMurray, for example?'

'Hugh? I don't understand.'

'I think I do,' I said. 'I think what the inspector is suggesting is that it was MacMurray in the study, imitating Sir Neville's voice.'

'Oh, I see,' said Rosamund. 'How odd! But then surely that would mean—'

She paused.

'I'm not very quick at understanding things,' she said slowly, 'but I think what you are saying is that you believe Hugh killed Neville while we were all playing Consequences and then pretended to be him when we spoke to him through the door. Is that correct?'

'I think that is what may have happened, yes,' replied the inspector gently.

'I don't believe it!' Rosamund said. She turned to me and grasped my hand and in her expression there was distress, with a hint of something else—relief, perhaps, that the solution had finally been discovered.

'Yes,' went on Jameson. 'I have been examining the scene again following Mr. MacMurray's admission that he was walking on the terrace during the game of Consequences and it is starting to look as though he may have played a clever trick on you.'

'But how did he do it?'

'I think what happened is that Mr. MacMurray went to the study shortly before ten o'clock and was admitted by Sir Neville, either through the door or through the French windows. I don't know what happened after that—whether there was an argument, or whether Mr. MacMurray had gone along there with the express intention of killing your husband. For myself, I think it was probably the former. Whatever the case, at some point in the succeeding few minutes he found himself with a dead body on his hands. He had to think fast. His only hope was to make it look like an accident. His first act was to ensure that the study door was locked, then he arranged the body as we found it, knocked over the fire-irons and, as a final touch, sprinkled whisky all over the place. Unfortunately for him, that whisky was a flourish too far, especially when he realized that his finger-prints would be all over the decanter and hastened to wipe it clean. That made us very suspicious, of course, since if it had been an accident, then the decanter ought to have had Sir Neville's finger-marks on it at the very least. Mr. MacMurray must have had a shock, Lady Strickland, when you came and knocked on the door but he quickly saw it as an opportunity. If he could convince you that Sir Neville was alive and well at a quarter to eleven and speaking to you through the door, then that would give him the perfect alibi. He imitated Sir Neville's voice as best he could, then left hurriedly through the French windows, wiping the door handle clean as he did so. He then entered the house through the side door, where he met you returning to the drawing-room.'

I caught my breath, astounded at the audacity of the whole plot, yet impressed at its simplicity. Of course that was how it had happened! How could we have been so blind? Angela had been right when she said that we had been misled into thinking that the murder had taken place at a certain time, but we had mistakenly thought that it must therefore have occurred after eleven o'clock, when in fact it had happened before half-past ten!

'I can hardly believe it,' said Rosamund, pale-faced, 'but if you say that's what happened then I suppose I shall *have* to believe it. Are you going to arrest Hugh?'

'We shall question him first,' replied Jameson, 'but yes, Lady Strickland, I believe we now have enough evidence to—'

He was interrupted by a loud knocking at the door, followed by the abrupt entrance of Hugh MacMurray himself.

'Er—Mr. MacMurray,' began the inspector, taken aback.

MacMurray jabbed his finger at Jameson.

'Look here, what's all this damned nonsense I've just been hearing about my shouting at people through doors and killing Neville?' he demanded.

CHAPTER FIFTEEN

WE STARED AT him in astonishment. How on earth could he have known what we had been talking about? MacMurray glared round at us.

'It's not true, I tell you!' he said. 'Why, the very idea is absurd!'

The inspector was the first to recover himself.

'I'm afraid I don't quite follow you,' he said politely.

'Oho, don't tell me you don't know what I'm talking about. I've just been speaking to Angela, who warned me that I was probably about to be arrested and that I should find myself a lawyer pronto.'

So that was how he had known. I had seen the realization dawn in Angela Marchmont's face when Hugh MacMurray had made the admission that he had missed the game of Consequences. She and Jameson must both have made the deduction about the study door at the same moment.

'Very well,' said Jameson. 'Yes, Mr. MacMurray, I will admit that there are some questions that I should like to ask you, although, as Mrs. Marchmont has already suggested, perhaps you would prefer to answer them in the presence of a solicitor.'

'I don't need a damned solicitor,' he replied. 'I'm innocent, I tell you. You slippery chaps shan't pin anything on me.'

He sat down grimly. Rosamund and I rose to leave.

'Hold on a moment,' said MacMurray. 'I want you both to stay as witnesses. I won't be trapped into saying something that's not true and I need you here to back me up. Please,' he added as an afterthought.

We glanced at each other uncomfortably and sat down again.

'Fire away,' MacMurray said to the inspector.

'Mr. MacMurray, in the drawing-room just now you said that you were not present during the game of Consequences which, according to the accounts of various people, began at shortly before ten o'clock and ended at about a quarter to eleven. According to Mr. Gale, you left the room a few minutes before the game began and we now know that you did not return until after it had finished. Will you tell me what you were doing during that period?'

'I don't know what time I left the room but I suppose if Gale says it was just before ten then it must have been. As I said before, I went for a walk on the terrace.'

'On such a cold, damp night? Rather an odd thing to do, don't you think?'

'Not especially. The drawing-room was too hot and bright and I wanted to clear my head—to get away and think about things.'

'Things? Do you mean the matter of Sir Neville's will?'
MacMurray reddened.

'Well, yes, as a matter of fact. But you've already asked me about that and I told you it was all rot about Myerson and me. I wanted to think of the best way to approach old Neville, to convince him that he'd got it wrong and get back into his good books. I don't mean in a mercenary kind of way—although I don't mind admitting that being written out of his will was a blow. I was very fond of the old man too, you know.'

'So you went out on the terrace to think about things. You did not go to Sir Neville's study first?'

'No, I went straight outside.'

Did you pass the outside of the study at all while you were walking on the terrace?'

'Yes—several times, in fact. I was walking up and down for some time.'

'Did you see Sir Neville through the window?'

'I didn't look through the window. It was in darkness anyway—I couldn't have seen anything if I'd tried.'

'Did you enter the study through the French windows?'

'No! I've told you, I went outside and walked to and fro on the terrace for a while. I didn't see Neville at all.'

'Mr. MacMurray, you must understand that you are in a very dangerous position at present. You had a very strong motive for murder, in that you knew you were about to be disinherited. Furthermore, you yourself have admitted that you were in the vicinity of the study at about the time we believe the crime must have been committed. The circumstantial evidence against you is very strong. In addition, although there were no conclusive finger-marks on the handle of the French windows, we have found a hand-print belonging to you on the glass, in just such a position as suggests that you rested your hand on one door while attempting to pull the other one open.'

This was a surprise; Jameson had never mentioned the fact before. MacMurray, who had been staring at his feet, looked up and gazed hollowly at the inspector.

'Now,' Jameson continued. 'You could have placed your hand on the French window at any time but the fact that we now know you were near the study at the fatal time is very suggestive. Shall I tell you what I think happened?'

MacMurray said nothing but continued to gaze at Jameson.

'I think that you walked out on the terrace for a while, wondering desperately how to persuade Sir Neville not to write you out of his will. You came to the French windows and paused for a moment, peering into the study. Then an idea came to you: why not strike whilst the iron was hot, so to speak? Mr. Pomfrey had already arrived with the new will papers and you had only a few hours to win round Sir Neville. It was now or never. You tried the door but it was fastened tight, so you knocked. Sir Neville came, saw who it was and admitted you. I don't know what happened after that—I suppose you argued, but found Sir Neville intractable and decided that the only way out of your difficulty was murder. Sir Neville was sitting at his desk. You picked up the African statue and hit Sir Neville over the head with it. He slumped forward. You then went to work: you wiped the statue and returned it to its place, then dragged the body across the room to the fireplace and staged the scene as we found it.'

'It's not true!' said MacMurray in a hoarse whisper. 'It's all a lie! Look, I'll admit I tried the French windows but they were locked and I couldn't get in. I looked in but the room was dark and I couldn't see anything, so I gave it up and went back into the house. I would never have killed old Neville—never, I tell you!'

His face had gone a ghastly shade of green and his hands were trembling.

Inspector Jameson stood up.

'Mr. MacMurray,' he said. 'I am arresting you on suspicion of the murder of Sir Neville Strickland. It is my duty to inform you that anything you say may be taken down and used as evidence.'

MacMurray took a deep breath and pulled himself together. He rose to his feet.

'All right then, I suppose you must do your duty. Must I be handcuffed?'

'Not if you are prepared to come along quietly,' replied the inspector. Far from being the stern representative of the law, he appeared not unsympathetic to his quarry's plight.

'Thank you,' said MacMurray. To my surprise, his demeanour was almost dignified.

We left the morning-room, to be greeted by Gwen, who came hurrying up.

'Oh Boopsie, what are they doing to you?' she cried.

MacMurray stopped.

'I'm afraid they're arresting me for Neville's murder, Gwen,' he said.

Gwen screamed.

'No! They mustn't! I shan't let them!' she said.

'Now then, old girl,' said her husband kindly. 'I shall be back in a jiffy when they realize they've got it all wrong, you'll see. But until then, you must be brave for my sake.'

He stooped and kissed her, then turned to the inspector.

'Shall we go?' he asked.

Gwen followed them out of the house, weeping. I turned to Rosamund.

'I wish we hadn't had to see all that. I feel rather shabby somehow, as though we oughtn't to have been watching.'

She turned away and made no answer.

'I must go and speak to Cook about dinner,' was all she said and hurried off. I understood. After the strain of the last hour, she wanted to take refuge in domestic matters.

Some time later I wandered disconsolately into the drawing -room, where I found Sylvia, Bobs and Angela Marchmont in animated conversation.

'Hallo, old chap. So they've got Hugh now, then, I see.' said Bobs. 'Come on, tell us all.'

I told them what had occurred.

'Oh, poor Hugh,' said Sylvia.

'Never mind "poor Hugh",' said Bobs. 'If a man resorts to murder and gets caught then he must face the consequences.'

'*Did* he do it, though?' said Angela. 'The evidence against him is very flimsy.'

'Why, of course he did it! I know you like to poke about and solve mysteries, Angela, but I think you're making too much of this one. There's no doubt he's the man. He was on the terrace outside the French windows at the right time—he's admitted as much—and you can't deny he had the strongest of motives. And then there's the fact that Simon saw him trying to get into the study in the middle of the night.'

'What?' I asked. Gale saw him that night?'

'Yes,' said Sylvia. 'He said he woke up and suddenly realized to his horror that he had left some of Neville's private papers in the library by mistake, so he went downstairs to fetch them and put them in a safe place. As he reached the bottom of the stairs he looked down the passage and saw Hugh standing outside the study in a rather suspicious manner.'

'What time was this?'

'Some time after two o'clock, he said.'

'But why on earth didn't he say anything before?'

'He didn't realize the significance of what he'd seen at first. Then later, as you know, he started to feel that the police were all against him and looking to fasten the blame on him, so he kept quiet as he didn't want to draw attention to the fact that he had been out of bed himself on the night that Neville died.'

'Did he tell you all this?' I asked, surprised. It seemed rather uncharacteristic of the reserved Simon.

'No, Joan wormed it out of him and told us. She's wondering whether to tell Inspector Jameson about it.'

'I suppose she'll have to. Or someone will. At any rate, that seems to clinch the question,' I said.

'Does it, though?' said Angela.

'What do you mean?' I asked.

'Why was he trying to get into the study that way?'

'Does it matter?' said Bobs. 'Probably he forgot something, or wanted to get another look at the new will. Perhaps he wanted to destroy it, even.'

'But he must surely have known that the study door was locked, since if he killed Neville he must have either checked it or locked it himself.'

'He must have forgotten,' said Bobs.

'That seems rather unlikely, even for Hugh,' said Angela. 'No, to me it looks as though he didn't know Neville was dead, and was trying to get into the study for reasons of his own— perhaps as you say, Bobs, to get a look at the will.'

'Well, I don't know why he was there,' said Bobs, 'but the fact that he was is jolly suspicious, and I'm sure the police will get the reason out of him one way or another.'

I tended to agree with Bobs. Each piece of evidence, though small, built up to a larger whole that implicated only one man. I thought Angela was looking too deeply for hidden meanings and was making things unduly complicated, when in reality things were quite simple: Hugh MacMurray, on hearing of Sir Neville's intention to disinherit him, had acted ruthlessly to prevent it and had covered up his tracks in a hurried and clumsy attempt to make the murder look like an accident. A sorry tale indeed, but why look further when the answer was there before our eyes?

Dinner was a sombre affair. Gwen, in particular, was unable to eat anything, so she sat there, gazing at nothing, for the duration of the meal. She looked terrible: tears had left tracks in her face-powder and her eyes were red-rimmed. She had certainly taken her husband's arrest very hard.

'Cheer up, Gwen,' said Bobs, at last. 'Hugh will be back with you in no time, you'll see. The police don't have a leg to stand on.'

Gwen turned her eyes on him.

'Do you think so?' she said dully.

'I'm sure of it. Now, eat up your dinner, there's a good girl. A wife oughtn't to let herself get too thin.'

She looked down at her plate.

'But they say they have evidence,' she said. 'They say that Hugh was the only person to go near the study that evening—'

She stopped and sat up, staring straight ahead.

'Darling, none of us really believe that Hugh had anything to do with it,' said Rosamund. 'Now you mustn't fret. I've called Mr. Pomfrey and he will go along and clear everything up. He's such a clever man that I know we can rely on him absolutely. Perhaps he can convince them it was an accident, which I really think it must have been, despite what the police say.'

'No!' said Gwen loudly, making us all jump. 'Don't pretend. Nobody really believes that, do they?' She glared round at us. 'I've seen you all, huddling in corners, whispering to each other about who you think did it, pointing your fingers. And now the police have fixed on Hugh as the most likely suspect, just because he happened to leave the room for a few minutes at the wrong time. Well, they're wrong. Hugh didn't do it. He couldn't have done it—he simply isn't capable. But I don't believe for one minute it was accidental.' She turned to look at Rosamund. 'You *say* you think it was an accident but you know it wasn't really, don't you?' she said sharply.

Rosamund looked startled for a second, then lowered her eyes.

'Ah!' said Gwen. There was a glint in her eye and her expression seemed to suggest that she had won some victory. She drew herself up.

'I know you all think I don't care a damn for Hugh, or for anyone but myself but it's not true,' she said fiercely. 'He's my husband and I won't let him hang, do you hear? I shall tell that policeman—I shall tell him—'

Before she could finish, she lost what little self-control she had left, burst into sobs and almost ran out of the room. Rosamund looked around the table with a worried expression on her face.

'Oh dear!' she exclaimed. 'Perhaps I should go to her. I should hate for her to do anything silly. She's not herself this evening.'

She excused herself hurriedly and followed Gwen out of the room.

'Bless my soul,' said Bobs. 'It looks as though Gwen has a heart that beats under that carapace after all.'

When the rest of us entered the drawing-room, we found Rosamund alone.

'Where's Gwen?' asked Joan.

'I've persuaded her to go to bed,' she replied. 'Poor darling, she truly is desperately unhappy about Hugh's arrest. I told her that of course we'll do everything we can to help him but I'm not sure she was listening.'

'Is that quite kind, Rosamund?' said Joan. 'I mean, I'm not sure you ought to be encouraging her to think that Hugh is going to get off scot-free. After all, things do look rather bad for him.'

Rosamund made no reply but rose and went to the window. She looked out into the darkness, a preoccupied expression on her face.

'Do you believe he did it, then?' asked Mrs. Marchmont of Joan.

Joan looked a little ashamed.

'Of course one hates to think of one's friends doing anything of the sort but—'

'His explanation of what he was doing out on the terrace was rather feeble,' I said. 'Why, he seemed to expect Jameson to believe that he went out there just to take the air. It was jolly cold that night, so why in heaven's name he should go outside to clear his head when he could have done that perfectly well in the conservatory or somewhere else, I don't know. And then there was the hand-print on the French window.'

'What did he say about that?' asked Angela.

'Just that he tried the handle but the door was locked. According to his story, he peered through the glass but it was dark and he couldn't see anything.'

'Not the most convincing explanation, I agree,' said Bobs soberly. 'Well, I must say it looks like it's curtains for old Hugh.'

'Oh, don't say that!' said Sylvia, distressed.

'Look at the facts though, old girl. Who had the most reason to kill Neville? Who was the only person found loitering by the French windows at the fatal hour? And who was fool enough to leave his hand-prints all over the place?'

'The hand-print doesn't prove anything,' said Sylvia. 'None of it proves anything.'

'But it all adds up and points very clearly to one person,' said her brother. 'That's right, isn't it, Angela? You're the detecting genius among us. What do you think?'

But Angela was frowning at something and appeared not to have heard.

'I beg your pardon, Bobs, what did you say?' she asked, rousing herself with some effort.

'I asked whether you don't think all the evidence points to Hugh's guilt.'

Mrs. Marchmont considered.

'It certainly seems to,' she said at last. 'But I was thinking of what Mr. Knox just said.'

'I?' I said. 'About MacMurray, you mean?'

'Yes. There was something—ah, it's gone now. A symptom of a brain declining with age, I'm afraid,' she said, smiling wryly. 'Never mind, perhaps it will come back to me. It was probably unimportant.'

I looked at her curiously.

'You seem unconvinced of MacMurray's guilt,' I said. 'You think he shouldn't have been arrested, then?'

'No—I wouldn't say that exactly,' she said. 'But after what has happened over the past few days my mind is in a whirl and I simply don't know what to think. Inspector Jameson is a very capable man and of course he had no choice but to arrest Hugh, given the circumstances.'

She would say no more on the subject but instead suggested a game of cards and we passed the rest of the evening quietly engaged in that pursuit.

CHAPTER SIXTEEN

THE NEXT MORNING, Joan burst into the breakfast-room with a wild look on her face just as Bobs and I were helping ourselves to a plateful of kidneys each.

'Whatever is the matter?' said Bobs.

'Gwen won't wake up!' she exclaimed. 'Her maid is having a fit of hysterics. I've sent for the doctor. Oh, I do hope we're not too late.'

'What?' Bobs and I cried together.

With one accord we hurried out of the room and followed Joan upstairs to the MacMurrays' room, where we found a smart maid sobbing loudly and wringing her hands and Angela Marchmont bending over the bed where Gwen lay, holding the unconscious woman's wrist.

'Is she alive?' asked Bobs.

'I think so—just,' replied Angela. 'But her pulse is very weak. I do hope the doctor comes soon.'

She cast her eyes around the room and they fell on a glass standing on a little table by the bed. She bent down and sniffed.

'Brandy, I should say,' she said.

I moved to pick up the glass and examine it but she shook her head quickly.

'I think it would be better not to touch that,' she said.

Her face was set, almost grim in its expression.

I remembered Rosamund's words of the previous evening. 'I should hate for her to do anything silly,' she had said. Had she suspected that it might come to this? That Gwen, distraught at Hugh's arrest and terrified that her part in the plot might come to light, would choose to take the easiest way out?

Just then, Rosamund entered the room.

'She's not—dead?' she asked, almost fearfully.

'No,' replied Angela, 'but I think it may be touch and go.'

'Do let me look after her while you go and have breakfast,' said Rosamund.

Angela shook her head.

'Oh but I insist. She is my guest, after all.'

'No, darling,' said Angela firmly. 'I shall stay with her until the doctor arrives. You go down with Mr. Knox and Joan and wait for Dr. Carter.'

Rosamund was reluctantly forced to give in.

'You thought this might happen, didn't you?' I said to Rosamund as we descended the stairs. 'You said she might do something silly, given her state of mind. I can't say I took the remark seriously but it looks as though you were right.'

'Oh yes, how dreadful!' she said. 'I did think she was behaving a little oddly but I don't think I really believed she would try to kill herself. She must have been driven to it in the desperation of her mind.'

Dr. Carter arrived shortly afterwards and was shown up to Gwen's room, whilst we all sat in the morning-room in a state of anxious suspense. Eventually, Angela Marchmont joined us.

'Well?' demanded Rosamund.

Angela shook her head.

'Things don't look good, I'm afraid,' she said. 'She is still unconscious and her pulse has become weaker. The doctor thinks she may be close to the end.'

We sat in shocked silence for a moment.

'Will—will she wake up at all?' asked Rosamund hesitantly.

'No. She is in a deep coma at present. Her maid is with her and is doing everything she can to make her comfortable. Poor Gwen will not be left alone for a second.'

'Did the doctor say what it was she took?' asked Sylvia.

'He thinks it was probably Veronal,' said Angela. 'There was a little bottle of the stuff in her dressing-case. Does anybody know whether she took it regularly?'

'Yes, she did,' said Rosamund. 'She had been having difficulty sleeping for several months, she told me.'

'Where did the brandy come from?'

'I gave it to her,' replied Rosamund. 'She was completely done in after what happened yesterday, so I poured her a glass. She drank some of it then said she would take the remainder up to bed.'

'Then she must have added the Veronal when she got to her room,' I said. 'I wonder whether she really intended to do herself harm, or whether it was an accident.'

'We may never know,' said Angela.

'Poor Gwen,' said Sylvia. There were tears in her eyes. 'Someone will have to tell Hugh.'

'Need he be told?' asked Joan. 'I mean, perhaps we ought to wait.' She did not say for what.

Rosamund left the room while the point was being decided. With no thought but that of lending her a sympathetic ear, I followed her and found her in the conservatory, absent-mindedly pulling the leaves off a rather ugly aspidistra. I thought how beautiful she looked, even in the midst of tragedy, her porcelain skin beautifully framed by her red-gold hair. She looked up and gave me a smile of the sort she used to give me in the old days, when I thought her smiles were for me alone.

'Dear Charles,' she said. 'You have been such a friend to me over these past few days. I don't know what I should have done without you.'

I took her hand.

'I'm awfully pleased if you think I've been of any help,' I said. 'But really, I don't see how one could have done anything differently.'

She gazed into my eyes and immediately it was as though eight years had melted away into nothingness.

'Why wouldn't you marry me, Rosamund?' I asked.

She smiled. She knew her power over me had never died; of course she did.

'Oh Charles,' she said. 'It would never have worked between us.'

'But I thought we were in love.'

'So we were but we were young and foolish and so *dreadfully* poor,' she said. 'Oh, I know they say love conquers all but is that really true? Does it conquer cold and ragged clothes and hunger and misery?'

'Then you had no faith in me? You didn't believe I should ever make my fortune.'

'Oh but I did. I had every faith in you. But I could never have gone with you to Africa, you know that, and to wait at home in England, trusting to an uncertain future, scraping to get by—I couldn't do that. I was weak, Charles, and you were much better off without me.'

I kept hold of her hand, still. I seemed to have lost my head.

'And now?'

'And now what?'

'Am I still better off without you?'

She gazed at me for an eternity. Her breath came fast.

'Oh yes,' she whispered.

'I don't believe you,' I said roughly, then took her in my arms and kissed her. For one long second she responded, then she shook herself free.

'Don't!' she exclaimed. 'Don't you understand? It's all too late now. Even if Neville had never been in the picture, surely you must see that things have changed. You've been away eight years, Charles. Why, that's practically a lifetime.'

'Not for me, it isn't. You are the same to me as you ever were.'
She shook her head.

'No,' she said. 'That's not true. I was never—what you thought I was. The Rosamund you thought you loved is a perfect creature of your imagination. She's not even human. But I—I'm a real human being, with faults and imperfections just like anybody else and I don't want to be loved by someone who would expect me to be a sort of goddess. I should only disappoint you, don't you see?'

'But—that kiss, Rosamund. Why would you kiss me like that if you didn't feel the same way about me as I do about you?'

She lowered her eyes but did not deny that she had responded.

'Perhaps it was a kind of nostalgia. Perhaps I was trying to imagine myself as I was eight years ago, before all this happened. Before Neville. Before—'

'Before what?'

'Nothing. I'm sorry, Charles. I never meant you to—I mean, I thought we were friends.'

'So did I,' I said.

'No, darling,' she said gently. 'It can't be that sort of friendship. You know that.'

'I *don't* know it,' I said.

She smiled sadly, turned away and left the room.

'Rosamund!' I called after her desperately. I started after her but was brought up short when I bumped into Sylvia. I begged her pardon in a somewhat distracted fashion and she smiled stiffly.

'What were you talking to Rosamund about?' she asked, in an unnaturally bright voice.

'I—nothing in particular,' I replied, taken aback.

'I see,' she said.

'Sylvia, I—'

'Really, it's quite all right,' she said, still in that same, high voice. She pressed her lips together and hurried away.

'Sylvia!' I exclaimed.

Had she overheard my interview with Rosamund? My mind was in a tumult and I could hardly think. What had I done? Had I behaved like a damned fool? Rosamund had always had that effect on me. I felt I needed to find a cool, quiet place to sit until my head cleared, and headed for the library. The room was empty but someone had obviously been in before me, as a newspaper and one or two other papers lay scattered on the desk. I glanced idly at the newspaper, which had been left open at the stock pages, but quickly cast it aside. My eye then fell on a scrap of paper containing a few scribbled notes. I pulled it towards me and stared at it in puzzlement. It appeared to be a list, although it made no sense to me. It read:

Why dark?
Arms
Dog
Keys

'What on earth—?' I murmured to myself. I was still gazing at it in astonishment when Angela Marchmont entered the room. She stopped as she caught sight of the paper in my hand.

'Oh!' she exclaimed, in confusion.

'Is this yours?' I said, embarrassed. 'I do beg your pardon but I couldn't help seeing it.' I held it out to her.

'Yes, it's mine,' she said. 'It's just some silly thoughts I was scribbling down before breakfast. I find the library is a good place to clear one's head.'

'So it is,' I agreed. I hesitated. 'It's none of my business of course, but may I ask—if I am correct in understanding this rather mysterious list, you are still thinking about Sir Neville's murder. Does that mean you don't think MacMurray did it? You seemed uncertain of his guilt yesterday.'

She toyed for a moment with the rings on her fingers.

'If only one knew what to do,' she said, almost to herself. 'Yes, Mr. Knox, after the events of this morning, it seems quite clear to me now that Hugh couldn't possibly have done it.'

'Events? Are you referring to Mrs. MacMurray?' I asked in surprise. 'But surely her attempt at suicide merely confirms that they were both in on it?'

'But why should she attempt suicide? Of course, there is strong circumstantial evidence against Hugh but there is no evidence at all against Gwen. The police have never suggested for a moment that she had any hand in the matter. Why, then, should she try to kill herself?'

'An upset in the balance of her mind caused by her husband's arrest?'

She shook her head.

'No, I'm afraid that simply won't do. Hugh has been arrested but who is to say whether he will be found guilty or even brought to trial? A thousand things could happen between now and then. There is no solid evidence that he was the guilty party, and I have the feeling the clever inspector knows it. In fact, I shouldn't be surprised if the only reason he arrested Hugh was to try and frighten him into a confession. There was every reason in the world for Gwen to be frantic with worry but none at all for her to try to do away with herself.'

'Then you think it wasn't suicide at all but attempted murder.' She nodded.

'But why should anybody want to kill her? Do you think she knew something?'

'Yes, that seems to be the only conclusion. I think she must have known or suspected who the real killer was.'

'Last night, she ran from the table saying that she was going to tell the inspector something,' I exclaimed, suddenly remembering. 'I wonder if that is what alerted the killer and spurred him to action.'

'Yes, I wondered that too,' she replied.

I was feeling more and more perplexed.

'But *who* was it?' I said. 'It seems as though first one, then another person has been eliminated. Soon there will be no-one left and I shall have to start suspecting myself!'

Angela smiled wryly.

'Yes, it does rather seem that way, doesn't it? The problem is the lack of evidence. Even if we suspect who did it, we have no proof.'

I looked at her curiously.

'I believe you know who did it,' I said.

She did not reply directly but picked up her list and began tearing it into tiny pieces.

'There was something I meant to ask you earlier about the night of Neville's murder,' she said.

'Go on,' I replied.

'I'd like to know more about what happened when you and Rosamund went along to the study and heard what you thought was Neville's voice through the door. The police think that it was Hugh speaking but if my theory is correct, he had nothing to do with it.'

'Then who could it have been?' I said. 'Everyone else was in the drawing-room—unless, of course, it was Sir Neville himself, as we originally thought.' I was intrigued: was Angela reverting to the earlier theory that the crime was committed after a quarter to eleven?

'Try and remember the voice, Mr. Knox,' said Angela. 'Who do you think it was?'

'Unfortunately, as I have already told the inspector, I don't remember hearing much at all. I certainly couldn't tell you who was speaking. I was listening to Rosamund's side of the conversation, if you see what I mean, and didn't hear whoever it was on the other side of the door.'

'Nothing at all?'

'I'm afraid not.'

'Ah,' she said. An odd sort of expression came over her face.

'I'm sorry I can't be of more help,' I said.

'On the contrary, you have been very helpful,' she said sadly.

I watched her as she drummed her fingers absently on the desk.

'It is difficult to know what to do,' she said at last. 'But I think I shall have a word with Rosamund. Perhaps she will help me.'

'You mean she might be able to tell you who was speaking through the door? I don't think she remembers any more than I do.'

'Well, we shall see,' she said.

She went off, passing Bobs as he entered the room.

'Hallo, old chap,' he said. 'This is a to-do, what?'

'You mean Gwen? Yes.'

'Funny that she should try to kill herself after old Hugh's arrest, isn't it?'

'As a matter of fact,' I replied, 'Mrs. Marchmont has just been telling me the most extraordinary thing.'

I told him about her theory. He whistled.

'I say!' he exclaimed. 'That rather puts the cat among the pigeons, what?'

'If it's true, then yes, it means we are back where we started.'

'I suppose it does.'

'I think Angela suspects who did it but she wouldn't tell me who it was. I don't suppose you have any ideas yourself?'

Bobs shrugged.

'No idea, I'm afraid. I was sure it was Gale but it seems I was wrong. I'm sure the police will catch whoever it was sooner or later.'

To my surprise, he seemed almost unconcerned. He picked up the newspaper and turned a page, then put it down again. His thoughts were clearly elsewhere.

'Something troubling you, old chap?' I asked.

He roused himself with an effort.

'Eh, what? Oh, no, no,' he said. 'I was just thinking of something, that's all. I was wondering when the police will allow us to leave, in fact.'

'But I thought Rosamund wanted us all to stay.'

He looked uncomfortable.

'Yes, dash it! That's just it. It's all very well for her to say that but it makes a chap feel a cad. I've told her that but she won't seem to listen.'

'What do you mean?'

'Well, it looks rather a shabby trick to be hanging about a woman when her husband has just died. Makes one look rather a vulture, don't you think?'

'I'm not sure I understand.'

'Of course, it's one thing when the man's alive and everybody accepts the situation in a civilized sort of fashion but it's quite another when he's lying there cold and dead and people are casting around for someone to pin the blame on.'

I looked at Bobs's sheepish face and felt the dawning of an awful realization loom upon me. 'Bobs, are you telling me that you—you and Rosamund—' I stopped, unable to go on.

Bobs uttered an incredulous laugh.

'Good heavens, Charles,' he said. 'You don't mean to say you didn't know?'

Chapter Seventeen

I SAT DOWN, my head reeling. What an imbecile I had been! How could I have been so blind? A hundred and one scenes from the past few days raced through my mind: a mysterious conversation at dinner; Rosamund's radiant look as she and Bobs returned from a walk together; a photograph in the newspaper—the meaning of them all suddenly became perfectly clear to me. Had everybody known about it except me? Of course, Sylvia must have known. It was inevitable—after all, Bobs was her brother and Rosamund her friend. Sir Neville, it appeared, had known and accepted it. The others probably suspected it if they did not know for certain. The remembrance of my own monstrous error of only a few minutes ago now flooded upon me and I felt the blood rush hot across my face. It already seemed as though I had ruined everything with Sylvia but would Rosamund tell Bobs what had happened too? Would they laugh about it together and joke about how poor old Charles had made an idiot of himself once again? I thought I understood, now, the cryptic remarks Sylvia had made on the first night of our stay here. I had been offended at the time but now it looked as though she had been right—I had been hopelessly, stupidly, absurdly naïve. What a mistake it had been to come to Sissingham! I had come here and knowingly laid myself open to Rosamund's influence, having convinced myself that I was too old and experienced in the ways of the world to fall for that kind of thing again. How wrong I had been!

Bobs was looking at me with an unsuspecting smile. I made an effort to speak.

'No,' I said. 'I must confess the news comes as a complete surprise to me.'

'You astound me,' he said. 'I hope you don't mind, old thing. I know you were engaged to her once, but of course that was a long time ago, and Rosamund was so fearfully keen to see you again when I told her that you had returned to England that I thought I'd better bring you along. Of course, the weekend didn't exactly turn out as planned, did it? Poor old stick-in-the-mud Neville. One can't help feeling sorry for him—dull and unwanted in life and soon-to-be-forgotten in death.'

I did not like the tone of his voice in talking about the dead man and frowned. He laughed.

'Poor old Charles!' he said affectionately. 'You always were one to back the losing team. Very well, I shan't wound your sensibilities any more. I shall merely say that he was highly respected and will be briefly missed.'

'Do you intend to marry Rosamund?' I found myself asking.

'I suppose so,' he said carelessly. 'Goodness knows, she spent long enough trying to convince Neville to give her a divorce. It would look rather bad on my part to drop the old girl now.'

'Was Sir Neville unwilling to grant her a divorce, then?'

'Oh, he agreed to it all right but kept putting it off for one reason or another. He seemed to think that the chaps at his club would look rather blackly on him if he detached himself from his wife. For my part, I don't know why he didn't bite the bullet and get it over with as quickly as possible, once he realized that she was determined to have her own way. There are plenty of people who don't give two hoots about that sort of thing. Never stand between a woman and what she wants, Charles, if you want any sort of a quiet life. I say, she is rather marvellous, though, don't you think? Can't you see her lording it over everybody when I inherit the title? She will be in her element, playing the *grande dame* and greeting the great and the good at Bucklands. That's far more her "thing" than sitting buried here in the middle of nowhere, with nobody but an elderly husband and a sulky child to talk to.'

I winced. This was too uncomfortably true. I realized now that even as a wealthy man I could never have provided Rosamund with the things she really wanted. Glory, prestige, the admiration of others, would never be mine. Bobs, on the other hand, would be the ideal husband: rich and good-looking, he liked nothing better than to be seen out and about, disporting himself in all the fashionable places and appearing in the society pages. And of course, following the death of his elder brother, he was now in line to inherit a viscountcy, together with a grand country seat and a house in Grosvenor Square. I had to admit that he was a far more attractive prospect than I—a nobody with a disgraced father and a murder trial behind him, almost more at home in the harsh heat of South Africa than in his native land.

'Anyway,' went on Bobs, 'you can see why things are a little awkward at present—I mean, what happens? The Young Pretender comes down for a weekend and the Old King very conveniently departs this earth under mysterious and suspicious circumstances. Elderly ladies and other persons of a more moral disposition than I might look rather askance on the whole thing, don't you think? I should myself, in fact, if it were someone else. And the Governor is likely to be a bore, too. I don't suppose he'd have been any too pleased at the scandal of my marrying a divorcée but that would be as nothing to a murder charge hanging over the head of his only remaining son. If I were he I should probably disinherit me outright, in favour of Sylvia.'

His tone was jocular but there was a furrow on his forehead which suggested he was more serious than he cared to admit.

'But why should the police fasten on you as a likely suspect?' I asked.

'Motive, my dear chap, motive,' he said simply. 'I wanted to marry Rosamund and Neville stood in the way—that's how they'll see it.'

'But you said that Sir Neville had agreed to a divorce.'

'In principle, yes, but as I said, he kept putting it off. In fact, he had been putting it off for so long that I shouldn't have been surprised if he had changed his mind at last. They'll say I became impatient and decided to act.'

'But you have an alibi,' I pointed out.

'So they say,' he said. 'But it rests on the word of one of the servants. Perhaps I paid the fellow a handsome sum to invent a story and save my own skin. Or perhaps I knew something to his disadvantage and was threatening to reveal the secret if he refused to help me.'

There was a strange gleam in his eye as he said it and in his demeanour altogether there was something I did not quite understand. Why was he so eager to include himself amongst the list of suspects in the murder of Sir Neville?

'I think you are worrying needlessly,' I said, 'but your course of action is quite clear to me. Rosamund needs you at present and it would be a low sort of trick to scoot off back to town now, leaving her to face all this alone.'

He laughed mirthlessly.

'A low sort of trick? I know for a certain fact that she would do exactly the same thing to me if the boot were on the other leg. She would never be silly enough to hang about and allow herself to get involved in a scandal if she could save her own skin.'

I could hardly believe my ears.

'How dare you insult Rosamund like that?' I demanded angrily.

'Because I know the woman well—almost as well as I know myself. We are as like as two peas, Charles. Why do you think we rub along so well together? We understand each other, she and I.'

I was becoming increasingly uncomfortable at the turn the conversation had taken.

'I don't think you understand her as well as you think you do,' I said stiffly. 'Remember, I was once engaged to her and the picture you paint is one I don't recognize at all.'

Bobs shrugged.

'Have it your own way,' he said. 'I suppose you're right about my staying at Sissingham for now, though.' He stood up and clapped me on the shoulder. 'Don't make the mistake of thinking that Rosamund is a frail little creature who can't look after herself, Charles,' he said. 'She's tough, that one. She needs to be, too.'

He then went out and I was left alone with my thoughts, which were anything but happy ones. I was horrified, angry, confused and embarrassed, all at the same time. Oh, how I wished I could go back in time and undo what I had done that morning! Or, better, that I had never come to Sissingham at all. It had led to nothing but misfortune and misery for myself and others. I was furious with Bobs: not only had he stolen the woman I had once—nay, still loved and made me look a fool in the process, he had spoken of her in a cavalier fashion that offended me and did a gross injustice to her. And yet this was the man she had chosen! Could she ever be happy with him? I felt I had been duped and betrayed by my childhood friend, who was only now beginning to show his true colours.

Of course, I had always known that Bobs occasionally took a morally dubious view of things but I had always put it down to natural high spirits, never thinking for a moment that he would ever do anything seriously wrong. I felt that I hardly knew the man. Was this what Sylvia had meant when she warned me that after having been away for eight years I might find that people had changed beyond recognition? Perhaps she had been wiser than I knew. I felt a stab of sorrow at the thought that Rosamund had trusted Bobs enough to place herself in his power. He had promised to marry her once she had freed herself from Sir Neville, but could she rely upon him to keep his promise? She had taken an enormous risk—one that involved the public shame of lengthy divorce proceedings with no guarantee of a husband at the end of it. It all seemed terribly uncertain to me. How, for example, did Bobs stand to gain from marrying a divorced woman? He was his own master but there was no denying that his family would be against the match given his future destiny as a peer of the realm. And there would be public disapproval, no doubt: the newspapers, for example, would surely have many things to say on the matter.

I am ashamed to say that at that moment, a thought began to form at the back of my mind—a thought which I quashed immediately but not before an insidious voice in my head had painted an all-too-clear picture of the much more lenient view the public would take of the heir to a viscountcy's marrying a widow rather than a divorcée. I put the idea firmly out of my mind. My oldest friend had disappointed me greatly, but I would not think *that* of him.

I drew myself up straight. My way forward was clear: I must fix things with Rosamund and try to restore our friendship to what it had been before my earlier blunder so that, when the time came—and I doubted not that it would—she should know that she could turn to me for help and succour. The best thing to do, I reflected, would be to write her a note. Having resolved upon a course of action, I immediately felt better. I should apologize for my clumsiness and take my leave to save embarrassment on both sides, whilst making it clear to her that I should be always at her disposal if she needed me. Then I should depart quietly from the house with as little fuss as possible, ready to return if needed. I took up a pen and paper and spent some time deep in thought, then wrote as follows:

My dearest Rosamund,

I write in the hope that you will forgive me for what I have done, although you could hardly be blamed for thinking it unforgiveable. Believe me, I should never, even in my wildest moments, have dreamt of acting as I did, had I not in my heart of hearts been convinced that my place was by your side. Now that I have had time to reflect, I can clearly see my mistake—it was very wrong of me to assume that the only thing standing in the way of our reunion was your husband. I failed completely to consider your own feelings and for that I beg your pardon.

And now, it seems that the only thing for me to do is to free you from my unwelcome presence, although of course this cannot wholly make amends for what I have done. When I am gone and you look back on the events of the past few days, I hope that you will think of me kindly as a friend—albeit a misguided one in so many ways.

Your devoted servant always,

Charles

I read it through and then signed it. It was short but to the point. I had never found it easy to express my thoughts on paper and rather than get tangled up in long, wordy phrases that might read badly and thus hinder my cause, I judged it wisest to be as brief as possible.

I had just sealed the envelope when the bell rang for lunch, so I decided to wait until after that meal before delivering the note and taking my departure. To my relief, Rosamund did not appear at the table, having sent word that she had a headache and intended to rest in her room for an hour or two. Angela Marchmont arrived a little late, as she had just come from Mrs. MacMurray's side. There had been no change in Gwen's condition, she said: she was still unconscious and being looked after by her maid and Dr. Carter. Mrs. Marchmont said little during the meal: her face wore a strangely dark expression, mingled with a hint of sadness. Bobs, meanwhile, was in fine spirits, which I felt was rather inappropriate given the presence of a dying woman in the house. As it was such a fine sunny day he wanted to get out of the house, he said, and suggested that he take Sylvia, Joan and Simon Gale out in his car for a tour of the countryside.

'The 'bus wants an airing,' he said, 'and I'm tired of sticking around the house all day. And I've never properly made it up to you, Gale, for running you into that ditch on our arrival. You must let me show you how a real motor goes—my word, it throws that old pile of rusty metal of Neville's into the shade.'

Gale looked somewhat alarmed, as well he might.

'I'm not sure that—' he began.

'Oh do let's, Simon,' said Joan. 'It's a beautiful day and it will do us all good to get out of the house. I'd like to forget my woes for a few hours and I'm sure you would too.'

'Yes, it sounds a marvellous idea,' agreed Sylvia. 'And don't worry about Bobs's driving, Simon. I shall undertake to ensure that he drives safely and that we return in one piece.'

'Once again, dear sister, I see the triumph of hope over experience in your eyes,' began Bobs, then stopped at a warning look from Sylvia, for Gale was beginning to turn rather white. 'Come now, I promise I shall conduct myself as one conveying a maiden aunt to prayer,' he went on hurriedly.

'Oh do come, Simon,' said Joan.

Gale was eventually persuaded that he would not be putting his life in mortal peril by getting into a motor-car with Bobs and after some bustle, the party set off cheerfully. Angela Marchmont had disappeared—I supposed to resume her vigil over Gwen MacMurray. For my account I was pleased, as it meant that I should be able to effect my own departure with little fanfare. I had decided that I should take the path over the fields to the station and send for my bags later, thus avoiding any awkward leave-taking scenes and maintaining at least some of my dignity.

I went upstairs and pushed my note under Rosamund's door, not without some trepidation, then repaired to my room to pack up my belongings. The house was silent, seemingly empty, and I was visited by a sudden desire to get out as soon as was humanly possible. Packing complete, I looked round to make sure I had not forgotten anything and remembered that I had left my pen in the library before lunch. It had belonged to my father and was one of the few mementoes I had of him, so I had no wish to lose it. I passed along the landing towards the stairs and, as I did so, thought I heard the sound of a door opening softly. I turned but saw nothing. Perhaps I had imagined it.

I hurried downstairs and made my way to the library, where I found my pen still lying on the desk. I put it in my pocket and was just about to leave when the door opened and someone entered. It was Rosamund.

CHAPTER EIGHTEEN

'HALLO,' I SAID awkwardly.

She said nothing but stood with her back to the door, eyes narrowed, as though calculating something.

'Angela says that Hugh didn't murder Neville at all, and that he will be released soon,' she said finally. 'Is that true?'

'I don't know,' I said. 'She did seem quite certain that he was innocent but I don't know why she thinks he will be released. Surely that depends on the police.'

'Do you think he did it?'

'I don't know what to think any more,' I replied frankly. 'First we thought it was an accident, then Gale went and made an ass of himself, then after all that MacMurray got himself arrested. And now Angela seems to think that Gwen didn't try to kill herself at all but was attacked by someone else, which means that our mysterious murderer is still at large. It seems as though we are all still under suspicion.'

'But they can't arrest anybody without proof, can they? That's the trouble with all this—there's no proof,' she said.

I nodded.

'It seems so,' I said. 'I think Hugh MacMurray was arrested pretty much on the strength of one hand-print and a weak alibi but of course any decent defence counsel will simply say that nobody knows when that hand-print was put there. He could have leant against the French windows at any time. There's nothing to say he did it on the night of the murder. My feeling is that the police arrested him in the hope of getting a confession out of him but if he doesn't oblige then they have nothing to build a case on. I am starting to think that this will never be solved, and that we will all remain under suspicion for the rest of our lives. It's damnable.'

'Yes. If only I could put all this behind me and begin afresh,' she murmured, almost as though talking to herself.

Her words reminded me of Bobs's revelation of that morning and my heart sank. I had forgotten that she and Bobs had already planned their future together, and that I should once more have to retreat into the background, overlooked and unthought-of.

'If there were only some proof, or even a confession, then there would be no more doubt, would there?' she went on in a louder tone.

'I suppose not,' I said, wondering what she was getting at.

Rosamund moved away from the door and advanced towards the desk, scrutinizing me closely, as though trying to read something in my face. I began to feel more and more puzzled. At length, she appeared to reach some kind of resolution.

She turned away, and her next words astounded me.

'Do the police know that you were tried for murder in South Africa?' she asked, picking a book from the shelf and leafing through its pages idly.

The suddenness of the question took my breath away, and for a moment I was unable to answer.

'How—how—' I stammered eventually.

'How did I know about that?' she said. 'That's what you want to know, isn't it? From Neville, of course.'

'He told you?'

'Well, not *exactly*,' she replied. 'You'll think it awful of me, but I just happened to find a telegram on his desk when I was rummaging one day. Your name caught my eye, and before I could stop myself I found I had read the whole thing!' She opened her eyes wide and smiled her most beguiling smile. 'Simply dreadful of me, wasn't it?'

She looked almost pleased.

'So,' she went on. 'Does the inspector know or not?'

'Yes,' I said, at last.

'Then he's spoken to you about it,' she said. 'What did he say? Didn't he think it suspicious? I mean, the fact that there's been a murder in the house, and that one of the guests was once tried for killing someone else?'

I started. Was it possible that Rosamund believed me capable of murdering her husband? I opened my mouth to protest, but she paid no heed.

'And of course, you had a very strong motive,' she said, lowering her eyes modestly. 'After all, you did tell me so yourself.'

'Rosamund!' I exclaimed.

'So they could hardly be blamed for thinking you did it, could they? Especially if some other evidence came to light.'

'What other evidence?'

She came forward and put her hand on my arm.

'Come, Charles, you don't need to pretend to me,' she said persuasively. 'You know what the police will say. They'll say that you were still in love with me and so you decided to put Neville out of the way. You went into the study, hit him on the head and rearranged his body to try and make it look as though he had fallen accidentally and hit his head. Of course, I knew nothing about it—I should have been horrified if I'd had any idea you were planning such a thing. Poor Neville! I see now that it was my own fault, for letting you think—well, perhaps I do lead people on a little. It's a very bad habit of mine, I know, but I do so like to be liked. Will you believe me, Charles, when I say I never meant this to happen?'

My legs felt suddenly weak. I could hardly believe my ears.

'You don't really believe that, surely,' I said, when I finally found my voice. 'You can't really think I killed Sir Neville— you, of all people.'

'Perhaps not. But it doesn't matter what I think, does it? If the police believe you did it and can find some evidence, then that's enough.'

'But that's ridiculous. There is no evidence.'

'Oh, you never know what might turn up,' she said vaguely.

'And,' I went on more firmly, 'I have an alibi, just as you do.'

'Yes, I do, don't I?' she said, as though the idea were a novel one. 'But I wonder how long it will take for the police to realize their mistake, now that they have decided Hugh is innocent.'

'What mistake?'

'Why, the time of the murder, of course! Once they see that it wasn't Hugh who did it, they'll realize that their times are all wrong. Then they'll turn their attention to you and me, Charles.'

'I'm afraid I don't understand.'

She gave a sigh of impatience.

'How slow you are sometimes! If it wasn't Hugh in the study impersonating Neville at a quarter to eleven, then who was it? That's what they'll be asking themselves.'

'Why, I don't know. It's a mystery, since everyone else is accounted for.'

'Yes, as you say, everyone is accounted for. They were all in the drawing-room at the time. The police know that.'

'So?'

'So, silly, that means that you and I are the next suspects. Don't you see? There's only our word for it that anybody spoke to us through the door at all. If you assume for a moment that we were wrong, or lying—and that's what the police will do— then there's no proof at all that Neville was still alive at a quarter to eleven. He could have died much earlier than that—at any time after about nine o'clock in fact, when he went to his study. And how many of us have an alibi for that period?'

'Oh,' I said, surprised, as I considered this new angle. 'I see what you mean. I don't remember exactly what I was doing, but I'm sure I left the drawing-room at least once. Other people probably did too. The police will have to start looking into all the alibis again.'

Rosamund shook her head.

'The only alibis they will look into are ours,' she said. 'Don't you understand? What motive could we possibly have for lying about hearing a voice in the study, if not a guilty one?'

'But Rosamund, that's absurd. Of course you made a mistake. Surely you can convince the inspector of what you heard through the door. We know now that I didn't hear anything, but surely *you* couldn't have been so badly mistaken.'

Rosamund looked at me pityingly.

'My dear idiot, of course I wasn't mistaken,' she said. 'Haven't you worked it out yet? There never was any voice through the door.'

I stared.

'But you said—'

'I know what I said, but it wasn't true, Charles. I was lying. I thought you would have realized that long ago, but it seems not.' She began to laugh. 'I knew it was a risky thing to do, but I never dreamed you would be taken in by it as beautifully as you were. Thank you, darling, for protecting me so innocently. You've been a great help to me.'

'A great help?' I repeated stupidly. My head was beginning to whirl.

'Of course. If it hadn't been for you backing me up, I should be the main suspect now, and that would be *such* a bore. I might even be in prison, and you know that would never do.'

'But, Rosamund, even if I hadn't supported your story, surely the police wouldn't suspect you of the murder?'

'Well they'd be awful fools if they didn't,' she said simply, 'since it was me who did it.'

There was a pause, then I laughed in disbelief.

'You oughtn't to joke about things like that,' I said. 'With the police snooping around, someone might overhear you and take it seriously.'

Rosamund regarded me thoughtfully.

'Do you know, Charles,' she said, 'I've often suspected you were blind where I was concerned, and now I see I was right. I wonder what I should have to do to make you believe anything bad of me.'

'What do you mean?'

'I mean, darling, that either you are frightfully stupid or I have been frightfully clever. And I'm not at all sure that it's the latter.'

'That's rather unkind of you,' I said, stung.

'Is it? I'm merely saying what I think. I'm trying to tell you the truth about what happened, and you won't believe me.'

'Of course I don't believe you,' I said.

She pouted.

'But I want to tell you about it. I've been bursting to tell someone about it for days, but there's no-one else to tell. Bobs would make a fuss and anyone else would go straight to the police. I know I can trust you not to say anything.'

'Bobs would make a fuss?' I was momentarily distracted at the mention of his name.

'Yes, of course,' she exclaimed. 'I know he's done some odd things in the past, but I think even he would raise his eyebrows at murder.'

'Rosamund, why didn't you tell me about you and Bobs?'

'I'm sorry, darling, but I thought everybody knew. I was sure Bobs would have told you, at least.'

'He didn't. Not until today, at any rate. And you let me go ahead and make a fool of myself,' I said bitterly.

'Perhaps, but you did it splendidly,' she replied with a laugh.

I was past laughing. I was depressed and humiliated and wanted nothing more than to leave as soon as possible.

'I must go,' I said.

'But you haven't heard how I killed Neville yet,' she said.

I stared, thunderstruck. Could it really be true?

'I thought you were joking,' I said.

'Of course I wasn't joking. What an extraordinary idea! But I must say I think I pulled it off rather well in the circumstances.'

'But how could you possibly have done it? There wasn't time. Even if, as you say, Sir Neville was killed before a quarter to eleven, I'm sure nobody left the room for more than a few minutes. Yes, I remember now—you were dancing with everybody that evening.'

'Yes, but that was afterwards. I did it before that.'

I looked at Rosamund, who appeared totally unconcerned at the enormity of her words, and a curious feeling of unreality stole over me.

'Suppose you tell me what happened,' I said slowly.

CHAPTER NINETEEN

ROSAMUND BRIGHTENED UP at once.

'How splendid! Where shall I start?' she said. 'At the very beginning, I suppose, when you went off to Africa and I married Neville. You do believe me, don't you, when I say I did love you for a time when we were engaged? I truly did, darling. But I simply *hated* being poor, and then Neville came along and fell in love with me and was rich, and I thought: why not? I'd struggled for so long and thought I deserved a little happiness, so I said yes when he asked me to marry him.

'It was great fun for the first year or two, as we had the house in town and there were parties and balls and lots of lovely things to do and I could see all my friends whenever I wanted. Neville was rather stuffy of course, but he didn't stand in my way at first—he didn't mind my going out if he wanted to stay at home, so I carried on having a gay time and was very happy.

'But then things started to change. Neville began talking about taxes and expenses and stocks and all those dull things that I've never understood, and started frowning whenever I showed him my cheque-book. He had plenty of money—you heard Mr. Pomfrey say so yourself—but he hated to spend it on frivolous things. He began hinting that I ought to spend a little less, and soon the hints got stronger and stronger. But really, darling, how can one spend less in London when there is so much to do? I simply couldn't live cheaply, which was what he wanted. I had a large circle of friends and acquaintances, and they all maintained a certain appearance. Why, it would have meant cutting myself off from them all, and I just couldn't bear to do that.

'Eventually Neville said that he was going to sell the London house and come to live permanently at Sissingham, in the middle of nowhere. He'd never liked London very much and I think he wanted to take me out of temptation's reach. Now, it was all very well coming down here for weekends during the shooting season—we had large parties of people and it was just as much fun as staying in town—but it was as dull as ditch-water having to live here all the time. So many of the really important people forgot about me when I was buried in the country, and half the time we had to make do with fusty old colonels and vicars' wives if we wanted to make up a party. Oh, I went up to London and stayed with friends sometimes, but it wasn't the same, because I couldn't be the hostess any more. It sounds awful of me, Charles, but I *do* like to be the centre of attention, and I missed seeing myself in the society pages of the newspapers.

'If it hadn't been for Bobs and Sylvia I should have gone mad very quickly. Bobs especially. But you know about that. It all started out as a bit of fun when we were living in town, but once things started to get a bit sticky with Neville, it became more serious. He started pestering me to ask Neville for a divorce. He said that as half the world knew what was going on anyway, Neville could hardly object and would do the decent thing like a gentleman. Then we could get married and I could move back to London and go back to my old life. My friends weren't the kind of people to be particular about a divorced woman, and anyway Bobs had such a high position in society that most people would have sense enough to forget about it.

'I laughed at him at first, but after a while I began to think: well, why shouldn't I? You might think it odd, but I truly felt that Neville had deceived me when he married me. After all, he knew what sort of person he was marrying and there had been an implicit understanding that he should let me have my own way in things and enjoy myself as much as I liked. And now, after only a few years, he wanted me to stop having fun and settle down miles from everyone.

'So eventually I plucked up the courage and spoke to Neville about it. Of course, he wasn't particularly pleased, but he had seen it coming, he said, and all in all was less difficult than I'd expected. He agreed to a divorce, but said he wanted to choose his own time, as there were various difficulties in the way at present—I can't remember what, exactly, something to do with business. It was always something to do with business.'

'But he never did give you a divorce,' I said, as she paused.

'No,' she said. 'There was always one reason or another why it wasn't the right time. He just kept putting it off and putting it off, and I began to get more and more impatient. I wanted to get away as soon as possible, and of course I couldn't expect Bobs to wait for me forever. At any rate, a few days ago I decided to take matters into my own hands. You see, we'd agreed that Neville would do the decent thing and take the blame, but as he didn't seem to want to do anything about it, I decided to tell him that if he was going to funk it then I was willing to admit it all and appear in court myself.'

'Did you tell Bobs?' I asked.

'Of course not! He would never have agreed to it. I didn't really expect Neville to agree to it either. I just thought it might spur him on a little. So, the other night, a few minutes after Neville had left the drawing-room, I went along to the study after him.'

She paused again and I held my breath, waiting.

'The door was locked so I knocked and said I wanted to speak to him, and he grumbled but let me in. He was in the middle of writing something or other and sat back down at his desk. I asked him when he was going to give me the divorce he promised, and said it wasn't fair of him to keep me waiting all this time. I was about to tell him that I was prepared to take the blame, when he interrupted me and said that he had been thinking about it, and had changed his mind—he wasn't going to give me a divorce after all. He said that he had been unwilling when I first asked him and had only agreed to it to please me, but that the more he thought about it, the less he wanted to be involved in such a scandal. He was sorry to make me unhappy, but his conscience wouldn't allow him to go ahead with it.

'Well, darling, you can imagine the shock it gave me to hear that! He had kept me waiting for years, and then just when I thought he *must* finally do something about it, he broke his promise. I started to protest, but immediately saw that he had made his mind up. And once Neville makes his mind up, there's simply nothing to be done—he's as obstinate as a mule.'

She sighed crossly.

'I don't quite know what happened next,' she went on, 'but I do know that I had picked up one of those dreadful African curios that he was so fond of, as somebody had put it back in the wrong place—one of the servants, I expect, while they were dusting. I was standing just behind him, idly looking at what he had been writing, and I remember thinking that he had just succeeded in ruining my life with a word. Then I found myself wondering what would happen if I gave him just a *little* knock on the head. It would be such a beautifully simple way of getting rid of him. Honestly, darling, I don't think I actually meant to *do* it for a second, but before I knew it there he was, slumped over the desk, quite dead! For a few minutes I hoped against hope that I had only knocked him out—which would have been bad enough—but there was a rather horrible dent in his head, and when I tried to sit him up he slipped sideways and fell out of his chair onto the floor, and then it was quite obvious that he wasn't going to wake up again.

'Of course, when I realized what I had done it threw me into quite a panic. All I could think was that I had ruined everything with Bobs, and that I should probably be hanged as a common murderess. My first instinct was to leave the study as quickly as possible and hope that nobody had noticed my absence from the drawing-room. I couldn't bear to look at him any longer, so I put out the lamp and ran out, taking the key and locking the door behind me. I hoped that nobody would try to disturb Neville while he was working, so I should have some time to try and decide what to do. The most sensible thing to start with seemed to be to go back to the drawing-room and be as entertaining as possible so that no-one would suspect me or worry about Neville's absence. Oh, Charles, can you imagine how I felt that evening, trying desperately to entertain my guests and to pretend nothing was wrong, when all the while Neville was lying dead in the study, killed by my hand! I was dreadfully afraid that Simon would want to go and get Neville to sign some papers, or that Joan would want him for something, or—or that *something* would go wrong and he would be discovered straightaway. Then, of course, it would be perfectly obvious that I'd done it.

'Once I'd calmed down a little, however, I began to think more clearly. I knew I should have to return to the study sooner or later—I understand the police can do terribly clever things with finger-prints these days, and mine would be all over that African statue—and I started to wonder whether it would be possible to make Neville's death look like an accident. I thought of the fireplace, and thought I might be able to drag him across the room with some difficulty, given enough time. Then I realized that if it was to look truly convincing, I should have to make it seem as though he had locked himself in the study. But how could I do that? I should have to leave the key on the inside of the study door, or it would look as though someone had got in or out that way. The only other way out was through the French windows—but the outside doors would be locked up at eleven, and I certainly wouldn't have time to do all that I needed to do before then, or you would all wonder where I was. For a few minutes I even considered doing it in the dead of night, then locking myself out of the house with the French window key and sneaking back in early the next morning, but of course that was an absurd idea and would be bound to lead to discovery.

'Then suddenly I remembered that Neville kept a spare set of keys to the house locked in his desk drawer, and that the key to the drawer was in his pocket. Of course! That meant I could go downstairs long after everybody else had gone to bed, arrange things to look like an accident, leave through the French windows and come back into the house through the side door. I would have to replace the keys in the drawer later, in case somebody remembered there was a spare set, but I was sure I could manage that without too much trouble. Once I'd thought of that, I began to breathe more easily—in fact I began to preen myself rather, on being so clever. Could you have believed, Charles, that throughout that game of Consequences, I was racking my brains, planning the best way to disguise a murder? But once I'd remembered the keys, I believe I enjoyed it as much as anyone. It was a very silly game, wasn't it?

'Of course, Joan almost ruined everything then by suggesting that we fetch Neville. For a moment I didn't know what to do. Then it occurred to me that this was the perfect opportunity to throw everybody off the scent even further. Why, all I had to do was go along to the study with a witness and pretend to speak to Neville through the door, and everybody would think he had still been alive and well at a quarter to eleven. As long as I didn't leave the drawing-room until the house was locked up, that would give me an alibi if anybody started looking too closely at the accident story. It was a risk, but one worth taking, I thought, as long as I was sure of convincing my witness.'

'And you picked me as the witness, as you thought I would be the easiest one to fool,' I said bitterly. 'Does everybody really think me such an idiot?'

She looked at me kindly.

'You're not an idiot at all, Charles,' she replied. 'But you do have the most beautifully unsuspecting nature. I knew it would be easy enough to make you believe that Neville really had spoken to me.'

She was right, of course. She knew that I had been so blinded and dizzied by her that she could have told me an elephant was trumpeting through the study door at us and I should have believed her. I felt sick.

'Go on,' I said, for want of anything else to say.

'Well, you know what happened next. I spoke to Neville and pretended that he had replied, then we returned to the drawing-room, bumping into Hugh on the way. Damn Hugh!' she exclaimed suddenly. 'Why on earth did he choose that time to go running around on the terrace, drawing attention to himself and raising suspicions about the time of death? If he hadn't done that, then the police would have eventually come to the conclusion that it must have been an accident after all, or that it was a mysterious intruder who did it. Instead they came up with all these clever theories about Hugh pretending to be Neville and then arrested him.'

'I should have thought you would have been pleased,' I said.

'Of course I wasn't pleased! Do you really think I'm such a monster as all that? The whole point was to avoid throwing suspicion onto anybody. When the inspector told me what he thought had happened I was horrified, but I couldn't see any way out of it short of confessing to the thing myself. There was simply nothing I could do.'

'You mean you left him to his fate,' I said.

'Oh, he would have got off, I'm sure,' she said. 'In fact, you said yourself that the police have admitted they have no evidence to back up their suspicions. Anyway, where was I?'

'We had just returned to the drawing-room with MacMurray,' I said, feeling more and more as though I were stumbling blindly through the most appalling nightmare.

'Oh yes. Well, we all went to bed, but I didn't go to sleep, of course. I sat up, waiting, until after two o'clock. Then when I judged that all was safe, I crept quietly downstairs and into the study. I had been half-hoping that I had imagined it all, but no, there he was, still lying on the floor by the desk. Thank goodness there wasn't any blood. The first thing I did was to drag him over to the fireplace. He was so awfully heavy that I felt as though my arms would be pulled out of their sockets. Then I knocked over the fire-irons to make it look as though Neville had done it when he fell, and filled a whisky glass and laid it down carefully on its side next to the body, holding it carefully with my handkerchief as I did so.

'I was standing by the door and had just started to wipe my finger-prints off the key when the most awful thing happened. There was a knock at the door, and someone tried the handle. I swear, darling, I almost died of fright. I simply froze and waited, thanking my stars that I had remembered to lock myself in. Whoever it was knocked again and said "Neville" in a low voice, so I assumed that meant I hadn't been seen, and that the person thought the light under the door meant Neville was working late.'

'That must have been MacMurray,' I said.

'Yes, Simon saw him, didn't he? At the time I had no idea who it was, but I was terrified. I held my breath and listened, and after a few moments heard footsteps walking away. Even then I waited for what seemed like an age before I dared breathe again and get on with it.

'I had meant to do everything carefully and calmly, but the fright I had just had made me lose my head, I think. Otherwise I'm sure I wouldn't have made so many mistakes. For instance, I was suddenly seized by the idea that one spilt glass of whisky wouldn't be nearly enough to convince anybody that Neville had fallen over because he'd been drinking, so in my panic I simply threw the stuff all over the place instead of picking up the decanter with a handkerchief, taking it outside and pouring it out carefully on the grass to make it look as though a lot had been drunk. I'm not sure what made me do it—I think I just had a mad idea that the place ought to reek of whisky. And it was very stupid of me to polish the decanter afterwards, I realize that now.

'What else? Oh yes, I had to clean the African statue. I picked it up and saw there were a few hairs clinging to it, so I scraped it carefully on the edge of the mantelpiece, to make it look as though Neville had hit his head there. Of course, Angela says that he was lying in the wrong position anyway, and couldn't possibly have fallen accidentally, but I didn't know that. I shall be much more careful next time.

'Once I was certain I had arranged everything as convincingly as possible, I got the desk key out of Neville's pocket, took the house keys from the drawer and locked the drawer again, in case anybody remembered the spare keys before I had had the chance to replace them. Then I unlocked and unbolted the French windows and left that way, wiping the handle as I went. I crept along the terrace and came back in quietly through the side door, locking it behind me. It wasn't until I was safely back in my room that I realized I hadn't locked the French windows, but it didn't worry me too much—I was sure nobody would notice, and I could always do it the next morning when I put the keys back.

'I didn't sleep a wink that night, as you can imagine. I lay awake, expecting that at any moment somebody would discover what had happened and raise the alarm, although of course that was absurd. It wasn't until morning that the hullabaloo started and I had to steel myself to play my part.

Mr. Pomfrey broke the news to me. He was very kind, but I couldn't afford to feel bad about that—the important thing was not to raise any suspicion. I pretended to allow the news to sink in, and then I was very calm and dignified, and told him that I should like to see Neville alone before the doctor arrived. He was unwilling, but as there was no question then that it had been anything other than an accident, he was forced to give in.

'As soon as I got in there I ran over to the desk, unlocked the drawer and replaced the keys, which had been wrapped in my handkerchief, then locked it up again and put the drawer key back into Neville's pocket. I see now that was a mistake to wipe them—just as it was a mistake to wipe the decanter, but as nobody ever suspected that that was how it had been done, it doesn't matter now. There was one terrible moment when the inspector started asking about the second set of keys and my heart leapt into my mouth, but he didn't pursue the question, to my relief.

'I was just about to run over and lock and bolt the French windows when Joan came in, in a great state, so I couldn't do it. At first I was scared, but once I'd had time to think about it I reflected that if the worst came to the worst and somebody noticed they were unlocked, it would be assumed either that they had been left open by accident, or that somebody had come in from outside. Nobody would ever think that it was someone in the house, because everything had been locked up at eleven.'

'But somebody did notice that they were unlocked,' I said.

'Oh yes, Angela,' said Rosamund. 'Why did she have to mention it? I do wish she hadn't said anything.'

'I think she wishes it too,' I said. 'She certainly intimated something of the sort, but Sylvia and I were there when she made the discovery, and Mr. Pomfrey and the doctor arrived shortly afterwards, and by that time it was impossible to hush it up.'

'Why on earth didn't I remember to lock them when I left?' burst out Rosamund in exasperation. 'Then everything would have been all right. Neville would have been locked safely in the study and nobody would have even dreamed that there was anything suspicious about his death. It would have been put down as an accident and nobody would have had any reason to look more closely into it.'

Despite myself, I could not help but agree with her. Angela had been right when she had said it was unpremeditated, but it had very nearly been the perfect crime. Rosamund's quick thinking had led us to believe that it must have been committed between a quarter to eleven and eleven o'clock, and we had all been puzzling over how it could have been carried out in such a short time. It had not occurred to anybody that in fact it could not, and that the murderer must have returned to the scene of the crime later that night in order to lay the false scent. It had certainly been an ingenious idea to take the second set of keys from the desk drawer and replace them the next day. Had there been time to lock the French windows too, then we should all have accepted the accident theory without question, and nobody would have spotted that the scene of the incident was somewhat unconvincing. The whole thing was brilliant in its simplicity—or would have been but for Hugh MacMurray's midnight visit to the study and Joan's interruption the next morning.

'But Rosamund, what about Gwen?' I asked. 'Was that you?'

She looked at me uncomprehendingly for a second.

'Oh! Yes, that was me too. Such a shame—I really didn't want to do it, but I had no choice. She saw me go into the study after dinner, you see.'

'Did she tell you so?'

'Yes. At first she didn't realize what it was that she'd seen, so said nothing. It was only later that she understood and confronted me with it. It was rather awkward, as I'd told the police I hadn't gone anywhere near the study that evening, at least not before I went along there with you. Didn't you hear her hinting about it last night at dinner? I was terrified she was going to come out with it in front of you all, but luckily she didn't.'

'She accused you after you followed her into the drawing-room, then?'

'Yes. She had somehow deduced that if Hugh wasn't responsible for the voice through the door, then you and I must have been lying about it and Neville could have been killed earlier. Since she had actually seen me going into the study she put two and two together and came to the conclusion that it must have been me who did it. And by the way, darling,' she went on, 'if someone like Gwen can make that deduction then the police certainly won't be far behind.'

'What did you say to her?'

'What could I say? I denied everything as charmingly as I could. I said that I had proof of who really did it, but that I couldn't tell her about it until I'd spoken to Inspector Jameson, as I was worried that the local police wanted to pin the crime on Hugh at all costs since he was the easy target and I didn't trust them not to tamper with the evidence. Of course it was a thin story, but it was the best I could come up with there and then, and she was so relieved at the prospect of Hugh being released that she swallowed it without question. I said I would tell her all about it the next day, but in the meantime I thought she ought to go to bed and get some sleep. I remembered that she had once told me that she took Veronal and luckily I happened to have some of the stuff about me— the doctor gave me some after Neville died, you know. I went over and poured her a brandy and put some of it in the glass, and she took it then went off to bed like a lamb.'

'That was a big risk to take. What if it hadn't worked?'

'I'm sure I should have thought of something, but I had nothing to lose, you know. She was threatening to tell the police—although if Hugh hadn't been arrested I'm sure she'd have tried to blackmail me instead. She's the type.'

At that moment the reality of it all finally dawned on me in a rush, and I felt my heart plummet into my boots. Bobs, Sylvia, even Rosamund herself—they had all been right, and now I had to admit it to myself. For eight years or more I had been nurturing a vision of Rosamund that was quite false. She was not the angelic creature of my imagination: in fact, she had proved herself to be quite the contrary. Had I not always known that she would never have stood for a life of poverty and insignificance? I had allowed her to abandon me, laughing, for a rich man whom she did not love, and yet for years afterwards I had continued to see her essential selfishness as somehow charming, as part of her appeal. What a fool I had been! And now here she was, telling me carelessly that she had murdered her husband because she was bored and he had refused to set her free to marry another, still richer man.

Rosamund was looking at me steadily.

'You have gone very pale,' she said. 'Have I shocked you terribly?'

I swallowed.

'I—I must confess that you have shaken me rather,' I managed finally. A thought came to me. 'But why did you tell me all this, Rosamund? What do you want me to do? Surely you can't expect me to keep quiet about it. For anything else you could rely on my discretion, but this—this is too much.'

'Yes, I expected you would say that,' she replied. 'And I knew you wouldn't want to keep it quiet, but don't worry—no-one will ever find out. I shall see to that.'

My mind was in a whirl and I did not understand what she meant at first.

'Then why did you tell me?' I repeated.

'Oh Charles, you know I was never any good at keeping a secret, and yet this was a secret that absolutely had to be kept! But I was bursting to tell somebody, so I chose you.'

As she spoke, she took a piece of paper out of her pocket and unfolded it. She held it out and I recognized it as the note I had written earlier—a lifetime ago now, it seemed.

'By the way, what did you mean by this?' she asked.

'Why, I meant what I said,' I replied, although I was not at all certain now that it was true. Did she think that the offer of friendship I had made in the note extended to keeping quiet about a murder?

'But what exactly *did* you say?'

I was becoming more and more puzzled.

'I don't understand. I said I was sorry for my mistake of this morning, and that I was going to leave the house to save further embarrassment for all concerned. In fact, I just came in here to find my pen, and then I should have left immediately.'

'Ah,' she nodded.

'Why do you ask?'

She laughed.

'You'll think it absurd of me, Charles,' she said, 'but my first thought on reading your note was that you were going to do something silly.'

'What on earth—do you mean kill myself?' I was astounded.

'Oh yes.' She looked down at the paper. '"And now, it seems that the only thing for me to do is to free you from my unwelcome presence,"' she read. '"When I am gone, I hope that you will think of me kindly." You must admit that does sound rather as though you were about to do away with yourself.'

I laughed incredulously at the thought that my simple words could have been taken in such a way.

'Of course I wasn't going to do away with myself,' I said. 'Why should I do that?'

'Yes, it did seem odd. The only reason I could think of was that you were so devastated at the idea of losing me that you didn't want to live any longer, but I didn't really believe that was possible. I know I'm conceited, darling, but even I don't normally expect men to go around killing themselves for the love of me. Still—'

She hesitated.

'Go on,' I said.

'Well, it did occur to me that your suicide would be rather convenient for me.'

CHAPTER TWENTY

I FELT MY blood run cold.

'What do you mean?' I asked.

'Don't you see? It would tie up everything so neatly. Everyone would think that it was you who killed Neville, then were overcome with remorse and took the easy way out! And this note would be the final proof.'

'That's ridiculous,' I said. My voice was an unnatural croak.

'Oh but it's not!' she said. 'It's such a beautiful plan, don't you think? Nobody could deny that you're the perfect suspect—especially since you've already been tried for murder in the past. Everyone knows that we were once engaged and that you were still in love with me. They'll think you wanted to get rid of Neville so that we could be together again. So you killed him, then later on came along to the study with me and pretended to hear his voice through the door so that we would all think he was still alive. Then you crept downstairs in the dead of night and rearranged things to make it look like an accident. A few days later I rejected your advances, and you killed yourself out of despair and remorse. Oh, it's perfect!'

She laughed and clapped her hands.

I could not believe my ears. Rosamund had just admitted to murdering her husband, and now she was twisting her own confession round to fit me!

I suddenly remembered something, and shook my head.

'It won't work,' I said. 'You have already told the police that you heard Sir Neville's voice through the study door. I told them I heard nothing.'

She waved her hand dismissively.

'I've already thought of that. I shall tell them that I must have been mistaken, and that I was just repeating what you had told me he said. At the time I had no reason not to believe you, of course, but I started to get suspicious when you changed your story later on and said that you hadn't heard anything at all.'

'Well then, how am I supposed to have got back into the house after leaving through the French windows?'

'Oh, I'm sure we'll think of something. Perhaps you stayed outside all night and then sneaked back in early the next morning, as I had thought of doing. Or perhaps there's a third key that we don't know of. I'm sure something can be arranged.'

'Don't be absurd, Rosamund. Nothing is going to be arranged. I have no intention of confessing to the murder of Sir Neville. Why, the very idea is ridiculous!'

'Angela knows, you know,' she said, as though I had not spoken. 'She came to me before lunch and said that Hugh was going to be released, and that it was time to put an end to this nonsense once and for all before anybody else got hurt, or arrested. She wanted to persuade me to confess. She said that they'd most likely be lenient with me but I don't see how they could be, do you?'

'Had she known it was you all along?'

'No, I don't think so. She had had her suspicions but was only convinced of it after I poisoned Gwen. She knew about the Veronal I got from Dr. Carter, you see.'

'What did you say?'

'Why, I denied everything, of course, and she had to go away in the end. I wanted time to think about what I should do next. I knew they wouldn't arrest me even if they suspected I did it. You see, there's still no *proof* of anything, and until they can find that then they can't arrest anybody. I went to my room to try and think things out. It seemed to me that the best thing for everyone would be for the police to go away leaving the mystery unsolved. That would be unsatisfactory but at least we should all be free, and that was the most important thing.'

'But then why did you come here to confess to me, Rosamund? As you say, the mystery would have most likely remained unsolved had you kept the secret to yourself.'

'Because you wrote me that note,' she said. 'As soon as I read it I knew it was the answer to all my prayers. Why, it solves everything.'

'I'm afraid I don't understand.'

'Don't you remember what you wrote? Here, take a look.'

She handed me the note and I glanced at it, uncomprehending.

'"I write in the hope that you will forgive me for what I have done, although you could hardly be blamed for thinking it unforgiveable", she quoted. 'Don't you see? You have as good as confessed to killing Neville. At least, that is how the police will see it.'

I laughed incredulously.

'Don't be absurd! That's not what I meant at all,' I said, but a feeling of dread ran through me. Could it be true? Could my attempt to excuse myself for having made those clumsy advances earlier be interpreted as an admission of something far more serious?

'It's not absurd at all. *I* know what you meant, but it's so beautifully vague that it could equally be taken as a confession by anyone else who read it. Oh, Charles, I can't tell you how delighted I was when I read it!'

I stared at her, aghast, the memory of the words I had written only that morning still fresh in my mind. She was right. I thought I had been begging her pardon for one thing, but anybody reading the note who knew nothing of the matter could easily interpret it in quite a different fashion—as a confession to murder, in fact.

'You seem to have forgotten one thing,' I said. 'I'm the one who wrote the letter, and can explain exactly what I meant by it.'

Then she smiled at me, and it was a terrible, beautiful smile.

'Ah, yes,' she said. 'But you won't be here to explain, will you? You must have realized that by now.'

I looked and saw that she had taken something out of her pocket, which she was examining with detached interest. It glinted in the afternoon light and was so small that at first I thought it must be a child's toy.

'It's a beautiful little thing, isn't it?' she said, when she saw me looking at it. 'Neville gave it to me a few years ago. I don't know why on earth he thought I should need a gun. Still, you never know when these things might come in useful.'

'Are—are you going to shoot me?' I managed at last.

'Of course I'm not going to shoot you!' she replied, eyes wide. 'You're one of my oldest and dearest friends. How could I possibly do such a thing? But—' she paused, as though searching for the right words. 'It would make me so very, very happy if you would do me this great favour—the greatest of favours, in fact.'

She walked slowly towards me and gazed into my eyes. The sunlight beamed through the window, turning her red-gold hair to flame and casting light upon her faultless complexion. At that moment, as she stood there in front of me, she was more beautiful than I had ever seen her, and I caught my breath. She took my hand and spoke, and as she did so I seemed to hear a buzzing in my ears as her words wove a spell around me, mesmerizing, captivating me.

How could I live, she said, knowing that the woman I loved was unattainable, was loved and possessed by another? What a glorious thing it would be to lay down my life for her, and for my best friend whom I had loved since childhood! She had never meant to kill her husband—of course she had not. It had been a huge mistake, and one for which she would have to pay with her life one way or another, unless I were brave and generous enough to come to her rescue. In the past eight years I had proved how bold and resourceful I was by going to Africa and attaining success and fortune. But in that country my character was forever stained by the disgrace of my trial for murder—and why should I want to return there anyway? It was a parched, barren place, devoid of life or interest. Nor would it do me any good to settle in England, as I should forever be reminded of the woman I had lost, and be forced to bear the pitying glances of my friends, which would not be lost upon me however much they tried to hide them. No, much better to end it all now, in the knowledge that by doing so I should be leaving great happiness and relief behind me. Better, surely, to die and be remembered for great things than to live forever under a cloud of misery and suspicion?

I cannot describe fully the effect her words had upon me, or why I should have been influenced in such a manner, but in some mysterious way she had bewitched and befuddled me into accepting her words as true. At that moment I really believed her when she said that my life had no value except as a currency to be exchanged for her own. How could I have thought otherwise? How could I have thought that she would ever be mine? She was too far above me and destined for much greater things which only I could make possible. I drew myself up a little. My purpose was clear. I had been called to Sissingham to make the ultimate sacrifice and save the woman I loved from an awful fate.

I felt her press something into my hand with a caress and looked down to see that it was the little pistol. I stared at it as her words went on, casting their hypnotic spell. I could no longer hear what she was saying, but it did not matter as I was no longer my own master and I felt myself nod in assent. Immediately, I began to experience the oddest floating sensation; it was almost as though my mind had detached itself from my body and was observing the whole scene from above. From my new vantage point I saw Rosamund indicate that I should sit down at the desk. My corporeal self obeyed, a dazed expression on its face. She gestured encouragingly. Was I imagining things, or was there a glint of cruel triumph in her eye? My mind, freed from its shackles, wanted to cry out a warning to my body down below, but no sound emerged. I watched helplessly as my earthly self slowly lifted the gun to its temple and prepared to squeeze the trigger. For one eternal second there was a terrible silence and time seemed to stand still, then all was noise and confusion as someone knocked my wrist upwards and firmly removed the gun from my hand. There was a shriek and the room was suddenly full of people and voices shouting and I was myself once more, sitting rooted to the spot and unable to act as Rosamund, screaming loudly, struggled with Inspector Jameson and a constable while Angela Marchmont vainly tried to persuade her to remain calm.

I don't remember what happened immediately after that, because all went dark.

CHAPTER TWENTY-ONE

I AWOKE TO find myself in bed, with Dr. Carter standing by my bedside.

'Ah, there you are!' he said jovially. 'That's quite a turn you had.' He grasped my wrist and took my pulse. 'Yes, yes, you'll do. A nip of brandy and some bed rest and you'll be as right as rain.'

'What happened?' I asked.

'I couldn't tell you,' he replied, 'but there's been some kind of a to-do with the police, that I do know. Angela Marchmont sent for me and said somebody had been taken ill, so here I am. Here, take this.'

I took the glass he offered me but did not drink.

'Where is everyone? Did you see Lady Strickland? Or Inspector Jameson?'

'No, there was only Mrs. Marchmont here when I arrived. Have they made an arrest, then? Who was it? You won't tell me,

I see. No doubt I shall find out in due course. Well, I'd better be off. Bed until tomorrow. I shall know if you've disobeyed me.'

He went off with a cheery goodbye and I was left to stare at the ceiling, dark thoughts my only companions, as the afternoon waned gradually into night. After a while I fell asleep.

I woke up the next morning feeling slightly better and half-wondering whether I had imagined the events of the day before. I got up and dressed, then descended the stairs warily, as I had no wish to be met by a crowd of people clamouring for information. The only person in the drawing-room was Angela, however. One look at her face was enough to tell me that I had not been imagining things.

'Oh, Mr. Knox,' she said. 'I hope you are feeling better.'

Her eyes were pink-rimmed but her demeanour was otherwise as calm and self-possessed as ever.

'I am, thank you. Where are the others?'

'Joan thought it might be best if they all went out again. They will be back later.'

'And Rosamund?' I asked.

'The police took her away,' she replied quietly.

'How—how was she?'

'Oh, she was quite resigned once she had accepted that there was no way out of it. Still, I don't suppose she will find prison very comfortable. I shall have to visit her as soon as they will let me.'

She might have been talking about a sick aunt who had been taken to hospital. She must have realized this herself, as she suddenly cried out uncharacteristically:

'Oh, Mr. Knox—Charles, what on earth have I done? I feel entirely to blame for all this. I am the one who stirred this whole thing up. Had I left well alone, none of it would have happened!'

All at once, I finally saw, in all its enormity, what Rosamund had done and how she had made fools of us all in pursuit of her own selfish gratification. I felt a rush of anger, which quickly receded as I saw Angela's anguished face.

'Of course you are not to blame. You were not the only person to suspect that Sir Neville's death was not an accident. Dr. Carter would have raised the alarm even if you had remained silent. If anyone should be blamed, it is I for my foolishness in believing every word Rosamund said and thus throwing obstacles in the way of the investigation. Throughout this whole thing one person after another has tried to tell me quite politely that I am an idiot, and now I find that they were right,' I finished bitterly.

Angela gave a small smile at that.

'Perhaps we should admit that we have both been idiots in one way or another,' she said.

But I could not smile.

'If I had only seen through Rosamund earlier, then perhaps at least one life could have been saved,' I said.

'Whose do you mean?'

'Why, Mrs. MacMurray.'

'Oh, Gwen, of course. Well, I suppose it can all come out now. You needn't worry about her, Charles. She is going to be quite all right. She woke up yesterday and is rather unwell but out of danger. Hugh is with her.'

'But I thought she had only a matter of hours to live.'

Angela looked apologetic.

'That was not entirely true. As soon as I realized that it was probably attempted murder rather than suicide, I told the doctor and we agreed to pretend that she was much sicker than she actually was. We didn't want the murderer making another attempt on her life, so we told everyone she was unconscious and that there was no hope of her waking again. But just to be on the safe side the doctor and Gwen's maid took turns to watch over her.'

'Of course! When she was found Rosamund wanted to stay with her while you went down to breakfast, but you refused to let her. Did you know then?'

Angela bowed her head.

'Then you have no reason to condemn yourself. All this has been Rosamund's doing. But you—you have been responsible for saving a life. *Two* lives, in fact,' I said. 'You saved mine, too. I am more ashamed and embarrassed than I can say at what I nearly allowed her to persuade me to, but I can never thank you enough for arriving in time to prevent it.'

Before she could reply, Inspector Jameson entered the room.

'Ah, Mr. Knox, I see you have recovered. Would you and Mrs. Marchmont care to join me in the morning-room for a few minutes? I have a few questions that I should like to ask, and it will be better, perhaps, to get this over with before your friends return, given the events of yesterday.'

His manner was not unsympathetic.

'Certainly,' replied Angela. She had quite recovered her composure.

'Now, Mrs. Marchmont,' said the inspector once we were seated, 'we owe Lady Strickland's arrest and Mr. Knox owes his life to your quick thinking, so if you please I should like to hear your story.'

'Very well,' said Angela, who had clearly been expecting a question of the sort. 'What exactly do you wish to know, inspector?'

'First of all, what made you suspect Lady Strickland?'

Angela sighed.

'It was such a small thing—something that Hugh said when you were questioning him about what he was doing out on the terrace that night. He said he had looked through the window but the study was in darkness. Now, if he were the murderer, we could safely disregard anything he said as a lie, but what if he were telling the truth? We all assumed that Neville was alive at that time, but in that case why should he be sitting in the dark? The only reason I could think of was that he was already dead and the murderer had put out the lamp—presumably to hide the body from view should anybody take it into his head to peer through the French windows. But if he were dead, then how could Rosamund and Charles possibly have heard him speaking through the study door at a quarter to eleven? Naturally they couldn't. The obvious conclusion, therefore, was that they were lying in order to make us think that Neville had died later on. And why should they do that? The inference was clear.'

'You suspected that we were in league together, then?' I asked.

'I'm afraid I did at first,' replied Angela. 'Not for long, though, as I remembered what you said that afternoon when we were all in the study. You were so very keen to call the police that it seemed unlikely that you had had a hand in it. It could have been a clever bluff, of course, but from what I had seen of you I thought you lacked—how can I put it? I thought you lacked the low cunning necessary for that.'

'I shall take that as a compliment,' I said.

'Do,' she assured me. 'At any rate, I had never been convinced of Hugh's guilt myself—and was doubly sure he was innocent once I heard about his attempt to get into the study in the middle of the night—so his insistence that the study was in darkness forced me to conclude reluctantly that Rosamund must have done it, or at least must have been the driving force behind it.

'You may be surprised to hear that I suspected my own cousin, to whom I had been so attached when we were young, but I know Rosamund, you see, and much as I love her I have never been blind to her faults. As a child she was beautiful and brilliant but she had a selfish, ruthless streak that was normally kept well-hidden, provided that she was not thwarted in any way. But sometimes her darker side would emerge. I remember once that, enraged at its refusal to obey her, she beat her own darling pet dog so hard that it had to be destroyed.'

'I remember you telling that story,' I said. 'But you said it had happened in New York and I had no idea you were referring to Rosamund.'

'Yes, I disguised the place but she was the child in the story,' Angela said. 'So you can see that to me, at least, the possibility of her having killed Neville was not as far-fetched as it might seem. And there was one other piece of evidence that pointed to her. Neville was a large, heavy man, and it would have been no easy task to drag his body across the room. Sure enough, when I thought back I remembered hearing Rosamund complain of stiffness and aching the next day. It was only a small thing, but suggestive. You may imagine that my thoughts on the matter were far from pleasant, but I could see no other solution.

'There were difficulties in the way of my theory, however, not least the fact that I couldn't see when exactly the crime could have been committed. I racked my brains, trying to remember what we had all been doing that evening. As far as I could recall, apart from the famous few minutes in which she went to the study with you, Charles, Rosamund had been absent from the room only once, shortly after dinner, but not for long enough to kill Neville and stage the scene. And I don't believe *you* left the room for long at all, which was another point that went in your favour. For some time I thought I must have got it all wrong, because I simply couldn't understand how she could have done it, but then I started thinking about the study being left in darkness and suddenly realized what it most likely meant.'

'I don't quite follow you,' said the inspector, as Angela paused.

'Why, it meant that the thing had taken place in two stages: the killing itself and the arrangement of things in the study to make it look like an accident. The more I thought about it, the more certain I became that no-one could possibly have done the whole thing in the early part of the evening before we all went to bed. But assuming for the moment that Rosamund was the guilty party, then she could have killed Neville during the short time she was out of the drawing-room just after dinner, turned out the light to make sure the crime was not discovered too early, and then returned later after we had all gone to bed, when she would have plenty of time to stage the scene.

'The difficulty with that is the problem we have all been puzzling over for days: how did Rosamund get back into the house afterwards? I still haven't solved that. I know there is a second set of keys in Neville's desk and it would have been easy enough for Rosamund to take the desk key from Neville's pocket and get them out of the drawer, which would solve the mystery of how she had got back into the house. But the keys were still in the drawer when the police searched the study, so perhaps there was another set we know nothing about.'

'No,' I said. 'She took the keys from Sir Neville's desk as you said. The next morning, when his body was discovered, she insisted on seeing him alone and replaced them quickly in the drawer. She had planned to lock the French windows too, since she had forgotten to do it the night before, but Joan came rushing in at that moment so they had to be left as they were.'

'Ah! Yes, of course,' she said. 'I should have thought of that. So there you have it. After Hugh was arrested I spent a bad night facing the very unwelcome fact that my own cousin was probably a murderer. The next morning we found Gwen had

been taken ill, and I knew I had to act. That's when I tele-
phoned you, inspector.'

'Yes, and it appears we arrived just in time to catch Lady
Strickland preparing for a final flourish. Mr. Knox has much
to thank you for.'

'I know it,' I said. 'Did you guess she was planning something then?'

'Not at all,' said Angela. 'It was pure chance that when the
inspector arrived we decided to have our consultation in the
library. When I opened the door we were confronted with the
most extraordinary scene. One or two moments were enough
to make it evident that there was not an instant to be lost. You
know what happened next.'

I felt myself reddening. Could I ever live down the events
of the past few days? I experienced a strong urge to leave the
country for a long holiday as soon as possible.

My companions tactfully forbore to dwell on the subject.

'I am very sorry about what has happened,' said the inspector, 'but you must see that I had no choice but to arrest your
cousin.'

'Oh, quite,' said Angela. 'One can't simply let someone off a
murder, however much it might upset her family. I only wish
I hadn't been quite so slow to reach my conclusions, as then
poor Gwen might have been spared her ordeal.'

'You were quicker than I was,' replied the inspector. 'I feel
I have failed rather on this case. But I should far rather be
shown up by an amateur than hang the wrong man, so please
accept my thanks.'

'Has she admitted it, then?'

'Yes, she spoke at length yesterday afternoon, and confessed to the whole thing. The solicitor, Mr. Pomfrey, was there, and I thought he should have an apoplectic fit.'

'How—how was she?' asked Angela.

Jameson thought a moment.

'Rueful and charming is how I should describe it,' he said. 'She accepted that the game was up, but was inclined to hope that a jury would take the romantic view and treat her sympathetically given her youth and beauty and her unhappiness in marriage.'

'I hope she doesn't intend to paint Neville as a cruel husband,' said Angela. 'She may not have loved him but he was never less than a gentleman and after all, she knew what he was when she married him.'

'Yes,' I said. 'That's only too true.'

Poor Sir Neville. I doubted that his character would emerge stainless following the trial. If Rosamund wanted to escape the hangman's noose her only hope now was to depict him as far worse than he was. Even then it was difficult to see how she could explain her attempt to put Gwen out of the way. And then there was her final effort to pin the whole thing on me. There was no doubt that she had intended my death too: on dressing that morning I had found a small bottle of Veronal in my bag, which she must have put there before following me down to the library. Had she been unable to persuade me to take my own life, I was perfectly sure that she would have taken matters into her own hands and used the gun on me herself. I shuddered, and once again hated myself for my stupidity.

'Still,' went on Angela. 'At least Hugh has been completely exonerated now and Gwen is recovering nicely by all accounts. Did you really believe he was guilty, inspector?'

'The evidence certainly pointed that way,' said Jameson. 'My personal feeling based on many years' experience was that he didn't seem the type, but one can't let personal feelings get in the way of the facts. If I did that I wouldn't get far in my job. No, he had a strong motive and was near the study at the time we originally thought the murder had been committed. Then there was the evidence of the hand-print, which suggested he had tried to enter the study through the French windows. One point in his favour, as you say, was the fact that he tried to get into the study in the middle of the night, but I didn't know about that until yesterday. I don't know what a jury would have made of it, either. Sneaking around in the dead of night rarely creates a good impression and a ruthless prosecution would undoubtedly make the most of it. And then there was his association with Clem Myerson, whose name is feared all over London. That was bound to come out. Yes,' he said, 'I think Mr. MacMurray can congratulate himself on a very lucky escape.'

And so can Bobs, I thought, but did not say it. I did not know whether Angela or the inspector knew about their affair, and had no wish to get my friend into further trouble.

'Silly, silly Rosamund,' said Angela sadly. 'Why did she have to do it?'

I was at a loss to explain it myself. Why had she been unable to be contented with her lot when she had drawn such a lucky hand in life? From whence had sprung the belief that whatever she wished for must be hers even if it meant removing people who stood in her way? The only person who could answer that was Rosamund herself, and she was at present under lock and key, discovering—perhaps for the first time— what it was to reap the consequences of her actions.

'I think after all this I should like to go away for a while to reflect upon my sins,' Angela said. 'I hear the Côte d'Azur is very pleasant in the winter. I believe there is a train.'

'So I understand,' said the inspector. 'But I should hate for you to think that you have any sins to reflect upon in this case. But for you two people might have died and an innocent man might have been hanged.'

'That may be so, but I can't help feeling that I ought to have stayed well out of it and resisted the urge to snoop. Had I done that, then perhaps the doctor and Mr. Pomfrey would have come to the conclusion eventually that there was no evidence that it was anything other than an accident.'

'But then Rosamund would have got away with murder,' I said.

Angela opened her mouth to say something but decided against it. I wondered if she had been going to say what I was thinking: would it have mattered? What if Rosamund *had* got away with it? If no suspicions had been raised, then presumably she would have married Bobs after a decent interval, thus attaining her heart's desire and presenting no further threat to anyone. Hugh and Gwen would have inherited the money they wanted, Angela would have been spared the knowledge that her cousin was a murderer and I—I should have retired discreetly to lick my wounds, illusions unshattered.

I shook myself. Murder could not go unpunished simply for everyone's convenience. The forces of the law were not to be subject to the whims of a murderer's family and friends, but were set in motion in order to right a dreadful wrong. And what if, having achieved what she wanted, Rosamund had one day decided that someone else was preventing her from having what she saw as rightfully hers? The events of the past few days had shown that she had no respect for the lives of others. Would she have killed again? We should never know.

'Well, I must go now,' said the inspector. 'Thank you once again, Mrs. Marchmont, for your help, and please do not think too hardly of yourself.'

'Thank you,' replied Angela. 'I shall try and take your advice.'

They left the room together, and I was left to my own sorry reflections. Angela might be able to forgive herself in time, but I thought I should never be able to shake off my own self-disgust.

CHAPTER TWENTY-TWO

I T WAS A crisp, bright, early January day when I next stood
on the quayside at Southampton, absorbing the bustle and
clamour around me. Despite all that had happened so recently,
I was surprised to find that I felt a little pang at the thought of
leaving England again. I had no idea how long I should be gone
—perhaps months or even years, and I could not help but regret the thought of abandoning so quickly what I had intended
should be my new life back in the Old Country.

The past few weeks had been difficult ones. The news could
not be suppressed and the whole of England had been abuzz
with talk of the sensational events at Sissingham Hall. Perhaps
only once in a century were the newspapers lucky enough to
get hold of such a story—the murder of a titled man by his
young and beautiful wife—and all the protagonists had found
their lives made rather difficult lately by reporters from pub-
lications that catered to the popular end of the market. Gwen
and Hugh MacMurray had clearly delighted in the attention:

their faces beamed out at me whenever I opened a paper, but for my part, I had spent several weeks dodging round corners and into doorways in order to avoid sharp-looking young men brandishing notebooks. For a man who wanted nothing more than to retire, bruised and alone, into a corner, this was no way to live and so I had decided the only thing to do was to go back to South Africa and immerse myself in business for a while. I should think about returning to England again once the uproar had died down and some other story had replaced the Sissingham tragedy in the mind of the public.

I stood for a little while, lost in thought, then shook myself and prepared to board the vessel, remembering as I did so the hearty welcome I had received from my dearest friend in this very place—a lifetime ago now, it seemed. If I regretted one thing more than anything else, it was the loss of that friend. I had not heard from Bobs since I left Sissingham, although a letter from Angela Marchmont told me that he had returned to Bucklands and was lying low at present. So far, the newspapers had not found out about his affair with Rosamund so it appeared that once more Bobs, that luckiest of men, had sailed near the wind and escaped. If the news were ever to get out though, it would do irreparable harm to his reputation. He had spoken lightly of the effect that his marrying Rosamund would have on his family, which was one of the oldest and most respected in the land, but he must surely have known the scandal and hurt it would cause and I did not believe that he was quite as careless of his parents' feelings as he claimed. I had thought of writing to him and had got as far as sitting down with pen and paper, but in the end had been unable to think of anything to say that would not make things worse. We had both loved the same woman and both been betrayed by her. What else was there to be said? And then there was Sylvia. I had liked her very much but Rosamund had stood between us and she knew it. How would she feel about my corresponding with Bobs on that subject? No, a discreet withdrawal on my part would be the best thing for all concerned.

'There you are, old thing,' said a voice behind me. 'Don't stand there dreaming. Better hurry up as we'll be sailing soon and we don't want to miss it.'

My heart leapt.

'Bobs!' I cried, turning. 'Why, what on earth are you doing here? And Sylvia!'

'Hallo, Charles,' said Sylvia.

The two of them stood before me. Sylvia looked rather serious and perhaps a little thinner than when I had last seen her, but Bobs's face wore the same expression of irrepressible cheeriness as ever. There was a moment or two of uncomfortable silence, then Bobs grinned and clapped me on the back.

'Bit of an awkward lull in the conversation there, what? Hardly surprising I suppose, given what happened last time I saw you. Still, forgive and forget, eh? We ought to thank our stars that nothing worse came of it.'

I felt my spirits lift and my face spread into a smile. I grasped his hand and wrung it heartily.

'Bobs, I can't tell you—' I stopped, lost for words.

'Steady now,' he said. 'You didn't think we'd let you go off all alone, did you? Not when you've demonstrated beyond all doubt that you can't be trusted to stay out of trouble when left to your own devices.'

I shook my head.

'I don't see how you can joke about it, Bobs,' I said. 'Especially not after—'

I paused, and he grew serious.

'Sorry, Charles. I suppose now's not the time. But you know I never was one to dwell on the more unpleasant aspects of the past. Chewing over it won't change what happened, will it? What's done is done and all that.'

'I wish I could follow your example,' I said. 'Perhaps I am too inclined to brood about things, but I don't see how one could do otherwise in this instance. Poor Rosamund.'

Bobs's face darkened and Sylvia bowed her head as we reflected on the last act of the drama in which we had all played such an unwilling part.

I should have known that Rosamund would never have stood for a life in captivity—or worse, allowed herself to be hanged. Once she knew the game was up there was only one thing to do by her lights. She had chosen her own way out and had taken it there in prison, with the help of the Veronal which Dr. Carter had so obligingly given her, and which she had somehow managed to smuggle into her cell. The news had been a blow, but after all that had occurred previously I was practically numb to further shocks. And perhaps it was for the best, as it saved the necessity of a trial which would show few of the witnesses in a favourable aspect. I was too disillusioned to suppose that she had done it for that reason, however. No,

I was sure that the idea of preserving her friends from public embarrassment had never crossed her mind. Her one idea had been to save herself from a tricky situation. Sweet, beautiful, terrible Rosamund. Her very memory would forever be inexpressibly painful to me, and I was impatient to get away and avoid all further mentions of her name, which in the past few weeks had been the only one on everyone's lips.

'Better go, Charles,' said Bobs. 'They've just given the all-aboard.'

'Well then, goodbye,' I said, holding out my hand.

'What do you mean, goodbye? You ass, hadn't you realized that I'm coming with you?'

'Coming with me?' I echoed stupidly.

'Of course! I thought you knew. Father wants me to go out and see how the land lies at this famous mine of yours. Between you and me, though, I think his real purpose in packing me off abroad is to keep me from getting into any more bad company here. After the past few weeks, I may have to concede that point.'

I saw Sylvia smile despite herself, and for the first time in many weeks I felt a glimmer of hope light up within me. If anyone could cheer me it was Bobs. I had not lost my oldest friend after all. The future was not as bleak as I had imagined. Perhaps one day I should even learn to forget.

'My dear fellow,' I began.

'Oh, never mind that rot,' he said hurriedly. 'I say! Hi! You there!'

He darted off after a porter. I gazed after him, then turned to Sylvia.

'No, I'm not coming,' she said in reply to my unspoken question, 'but I shall write, if you like.'

'I should like it very much,' I said sincerely. 'Sylvia—'

'I'm very sorry about what happened,' she said quickly, 'and I want you to know that I'm not angry with you. I can't blame you, I suppose. Rosamund was always the star-turn; I knew that. We all knew it.'

'The more fool I for being blinded,' I said. 'Will you believe me when I say that it was a brief infatuation, a moment of madness?'

'No,' she said, smiling sadly, and I was silenced. She was right, of course, and it was unfair of me to try and convince her otherwise.

An increase in the bustle around us indicated that it was time to go.

'Shall you come and visit us?' I asked. Now it came to the point, I was unwilling to take leave.

'I believe I shall,' she replied. 'Mother and Father want to go, and I dare say they'll let me tag along.' She shivered. 'Anything to escape this beastly cold. Well, goodbye.'

She held out her hand and I raised it to my lips, then turned and went to join Bobs, who was standing at the foot of the gang-plank, waiting.

'All aboard, then,' he said. 'I warn you now, I know nothing about this business of yours, so I shall be relying on you to teach me all about it.'

I looked back. Sylvia was still standing there, her hair gleaming in the low winter sunlight. She waved, then turned on her heel and walked off. I found I was already looking forward to seeing her again.

'Shall we go?' I said to Bobs, and we turned and walked up the gang-plank together.

NEW RELEASES

If you'd like to receive news of further releases by Clara Benson, you can sign up to my mailing list here: smarturl.it/ClaraBenson.

We take data confidentiality very seriously and will not pass your details on to anybody else or send you any spam.

ClaraBenson.com

BOOKS IN THIS SERIES

- The Murder at Sissingham Hall
- The Mystery at Underwood House
- The Treasure at Poldarrow Point
- The Riddle at Gipsy's Mile
- The Incident at Fives Castle
- The Imbroglio at the Villa Pozzi
- The Problem at Two Tithes
- The Trouble at Wakeley Court
- The Scandal at 23 Mount Street
- The Shadow at Greystone Chase

Made in the USA
San Bernardino, CA
07 April 2019